IT'S GOING TO BE A KILLER YEAR!

Is the senior class at Shadyside High doomed? That's the prediction Trisha Conrad makes at her summer party—and it looks as if she may be right. Spend a year with the FEAR STREET seniors, as each month in this new 12-book series brings horror after horror. Will anyone reach graduation day alive?

Only R.L. Stine knows...

SHADYSIDE HIGH YEARBOOK

Mira Block

LIKES:
Going to clubs, guys in bands, sexy clothes

REMEMBERS:
The cemetery, senior camp-out, hanging out with Clarissa

HATES:
Waifs, talking on the phone, psychics

QUOTE:
"Don't hate me 'cause I'm beautiful."

Greta Bradley

LIKES:
Cheerleading, [illegible] at my [illegible]

REMEMBERS:
The first time [illegible] me out, shopping at Chanel with Jade

HATES:
Ceramics, creepy houses, [illegible]

REST IN PEACE

QUOTE:
"That boy is mine."

Trisha Conrad

LIKES:
Shopping in the mall my dad owns, giving fabulous parties, Gary Fresno

REMEMBERS:
The murder game, the senior table at Pete's Pizza

HATES:
Rich girl jokes, bad karma, overalls

QUOTE:
"What you don't know will hurt you."

Danielle Cortez

LIKES:
My [illegible] the Tigers, dancing

REMEMBERS:
Trisha's big party, finally making varsity cheerleader

HATES:
The first day of [illegible] cold [illegible]

REST IN PEACE

QUOTE:
"Push 'em down, push 'em down, push 'em waaaay down! Go Tigers!"

Clark Dickson

LIKES:
Debra Lake, poetry, painting

REMEMBERS:
Trisha's party, the first time I saw Debra

HATES:
Nicknames, dentists, garlic pizza, tans

QUOTE:
"Fangs for the memories."

Jennifer Fear

LIKES:
Basketball, antique jewelry, cool music

REMEMBERS:
The doom spell, senior cut day, hanging with Trisha and Josie

HATES:
The way people are afraid of the Fears, pierced eyebrows

QUOTE:
"There's nothing to fear but fear itself."

Jade Feldman

LIKES:
Cheerleading, expensive clothes, working out

REMEMBERS:
ice cream pig-outs with Dana

HATES:
Cheerleading captains, gossip, SAT courses

QUOTE:
"You get what you pay for."

REST IN PEACE

Gary Fresno

LIKES:
Hanging out, babes, cutting classes, napping in class everyday

REMEMBERS:
Cruisin' Division Street with the guys, that special night with that special person (you know who you are...)

HATES:
My beat-up Civic, working after school everyday, cops

QUOTE:
"Don't judge a book by its cover."

REST IN PEACE

Kenny Klein

LIKES:
Jade Feldman, chemistry, Latin, baseball

REMEMBERS:
The first time I beat Marla Newman in a debate, Junior Prom with Jade

HATES:
Nine-year-olds who like to torture camp counselors, cafeteria food

QUOTE:
"Look before you leap."

Debra Lake

LIKES:
Sensitive guys, Clark's poetry

REMEMBERS:
Basketball games, when Clark painted my portrait

HATES:
Possessive boyfriends and jealous girlfriends

QUOTE:
"I would do anything for you, but I won't do that."

Stacy Malcolm

LIKES:
Sports, funky hats, shopping

REMEMBERS:
Running laps with Mary, stuffing our faces at Pete's, Mr. Morley and Rob

HATES:
Psycho killers, stealing boyfriends

QUOTE:
"College, here I come!"

Josh Maxwell

LIKES:
Debra Lake, Debra Lake, Debra Lake

REMEMBERS:
Hanging out at the old mill, senior camp-out, Coach's pep talks

HATES:
Funeral homes, driving my parents' car, tomato juice

QUOTE:
"Sometimes you don't realize the truth until it bites you right on the neck."

Josie Maxwell

LIKES:
Black clothes, black nail polish, black lipstick, photography

REMEMBERS:
Trisha's first senior party, the memorial wall

HATES:
Algebra, evil spirits (including Marla Newman), being compared to my stepbrother Josh

QUOTE:
"The past isn't always the past—sometimes it's the future."

Mickey Myers

LIKES:
Jammin' with the band, partying, hot girls

REMEMBERS:
Swimming in Fear Lake, the storm, my first gig at the Underground

HATES:
Dweebs, studying, girls who diet, station wagons

QUOTE:
"Shadyside High rules!"

Marla Newman

LIKES:
Writing, cool clothes, _____

REMEMBERS:
Yearbook committee, competing with Kenny Klein, when Josie put a spell on me (ha ha)

HATES:
Girls who wear all black, guys with long hair, the dark arts

QUOTE:
"The power is divided when the circle is not round."

REST IN PEACE

Mary O'Connor

LIKES:
Running, ripped jeans, hair spray

REMEMBERS:
Not being invited to Trisha's party, rat poison

HATES:
Social studies, rich girls, cliques

QUOTE:
"Just say no."

Dana Palmer

LIKES:
Boys, boys, boys, cheerleading, short skirts

REMEMBERS:
Senior camp-out with Mickey, Homecoming, the back seat

HATES:
Private cheerleading performances, fire batons, sharing clothes

QUOTE:
"The bad twin always wins!"

Deirdre Palmer

LIKES:
Myst... good clothes, old movies

REMEMBERS:
The cabin in the Fear Street woods, sleepovers at Jen's

HATES:
Being a "good girl," wet socks

QUOTE:
"What you see isn't always what you get."

REST IN PEACE

Will Reynolds

LIKES:
The Turner family, playing guitar, clubbing

REMEMBERS:
The first time Clarissa saw me without my dreads, our booth at Pete's

HATES:
Lite FM, the clinic, lilacs

QUOTE:
"I get knocked down, but I get up again..."

Ty Sullivan

LIKES:
Cheerleaders, ...ts, ...ars, psychics, brains, football

REMEMBERS:
The graveyard wi... kn... ...n... Ken... ...n's lucky shot

HATES:
Painting fe...s, Valentine's Day

QUOTE:
"The more the merrier."

REST IN PEACE

Justin Thompson

LIKES:
~~In~~ ~~per~~ ~~special~~ ~~person~~ ~~the~~ Beastie Boys, Barry White

REMEMBERS:
Don't want to remember anything from Shadyside

HATES:
Having my face dunked in the toilet, being chased by Ty and Gary

QUOTE:
"You're my everything."

Clarissa Turner

LIKES:
Art, music, talking on the phone

REMEMBERS:
Shopping with Debra, my first day back to school, eating pizza with Will

HATES:
Mlra Block

QUOTE:
"Real friendship never dies."

Matty Winger

LIKES:
Computers, video games, Star Trek

REMEMBERS:
The murder game—good one Trisha

HATES:
People who can't take a joke, finding Clark's cape with Josh

QUOTE:
"Don't worry, be happy."

Phoebe Yamura

LIKES:
Cheerleading, gymnastics, big crowds

REMEMBERS:
That awesome game against Waynesbridge, senior trip, tailgate parties

HATES:
When people don't give it their all, liars, vans

QUOTE:
"Today is the first day of the rest of our lives."

R.L. Stine
Seniors
a FEAR STREET® Super Chiller

Graduation
episode twelve **Day**

A Parachute Press Book

A GOLD KEY PAPERBACK
Golden Books Publishing Company, Inc.
New York

Check out the new FEAR STREET® Website
http://www.fearstreet.com

A Gold Key Paperback Original

Golden Books Publishing Company, Inc.
888 Seventh Avenue
New York, NY 10106

ISBN: 0-307-24716-3

First Gold Key paperback printing June 1999

10   9   8   7   6   5   4   3   2   1

Photographer: Jimmy Levin

Printed in the U.S.A.

Graduation Day

Prologue

Josie Maxwell squeezed Jennifer Fear's hand. "I'm totally psyched!" she exclaimed, tossing back her straight black hair.

Jennifer frowned at her friend. "I never knew you were such a shopping freak."

Josie gazed down the rows of skirts and tops and dresses. "I need something really sexy. Something to make everyone wish they hadn't ignored me all year." A bitter laugh escaped her throat.

Jennifer reacted with surprise. "Hey—don't look at me. I didn't ignore you, Josie."

Josie examined a silky black miniskirt. "I know. You're a good friend. I—I guess I want this graduation party to make up for everything. Everything horrible that happened this year. I want to dance and laugh and look great and—"

She let the skirt fall back into place on the rack and turned. "Jennifer—?"

Josie squinted into the bright fluorescent light of the boutique. Her eyes scanned the rows of clothing racks. "Hey—!"

Where had Jennifer disappeared to?

"Jen—find anything good? I want something bright. Red, maybe. No. Silver. Jen?"

No reply.

Josie turned to the front of the store. No one at the counter. No salespeople in the narrow aisles.

Silence.

Her eyes swept over a long rack of brightly colored skirts. Behind it, a table stacked high with T-shirts. She backed up, into a rack of black and gray dresses.

"Jen—? Where'd you go?"

A bright flash of light—like a thousand cameras going off at once—made Josie gasp. She shut her eyes and rubbed them, trying to rub away the pain.

Her head throbbed as she opened her eyes. And squinted into a hazy blur. She blinked several times, struggling to focus.

Finally the long clothing racks shimmered back into view.

Red. Everything red?

"No—!" Josie uttered a startled cry.

She grabbed the gown in front of her. Not a gown. A robe.

A red graduation robe.

A whole rack of red graduation robes.

"No—wait—" she murmured, her head spinning in confusion.

The brightly colored skirts all gone. The T-shirts all vanished.

Replaced by row after row of red robes.

I've got to get out, Josie thought, feeling a wave of panic sweep down her body, tightening her throat, making her legs tremble.

"Got to get out!"

She took a lurching step toward the door.

Something sticky. Her shoe stuck to the floor.

She lowered her gaze—and gasped.

At first she thought she was standing on one of the red robes. It took a few seconds to recognize the blood.

A thick, dark pool of blood.

"No . . . no . . . please . . ."

She took another sticky step. The thick blood splashed up over the sides of her shoes.

"No . . . please . . ."

Too much horror already, she thought. I can't take any more of this.

"Jen—? Are you still here? Help me, Jen. Help get me out of here!"

She heard trickling. Splashing.

And saw blood flowing down the fronts of the robes. A spreading puddle of blood beneath each graduation robe.

The robes shuffled on the racks, as if people were inside them. As Josie gaped in horror, the blood poured down the twisting, trembling robes.

"Jennifer—help me!"

A yellowed skull popped up in a robe across from her. Josie fell back, her shoes sticking in the puddle of blood on the floor. The skull opened its jaws in a toothless grin.

Another skull appeared in the open neck of the next robe. Another.

Another . . . Until Josie stared at an endless row of grinning skulls in bleeding graduation gowns.

Red . . . a steaming river of red . . .

It shimmered and bubbled until it filled her eyes.

Josie woke up from her nightmare and sat straight up in bed, her heart pounding. Her nightshirt stuck wetly to her back.

She sucked in breath after breath, waiting for her heartbeat to slow.

I knew it was a dream, she thought. I knew all along that it was just a hideous dream.

But was it also a message?

"No one will survive graduation," she murmured in a trembling whisper. "We're all going to die . . . All of us. And it's all *my fault.*"

4

PART ONE

Chapter One

Say "Cheese"

Josie pawed through her bag until she found a hairbrush. Then, using the window as a mirror, she began brushing out her shoulder-length dark hair.

"Hey, Jos—"

She turned at the sound of the familiar voice and gazed at her stepbrother, Josh, who poked his head into the doorway.

"I thought you were coming home," Josh said, adjusting a Shadyside High baseball cap over his dark hair.

"No way," Josie replied, turning back to the window and starting to brush a new part in the middle of her hair. "I'm waiting for the yearbooks to arrive."

In the window reflection she saw Josh pull off the cap, bend the bill, and return it to his head. Why did he bother with the cap? she wondered. He never could get it the way he wanted it. And he looked so junior high in it, anyway.

"Yearbooks coming today?" he asked.

Stacy Malcolm pushed past Josh into the yearbook office. "That's what the printer said," she told Josh. "The truck is on its way."

"Want to stay and see them?" Josie asked, frowning at her reflection. Her reflection frowned back at her.

"No, thanks. Just pictures of a lot of dead people," Josh muttered.

Josie spun around. "Well, you're Mister Sensitive today!" she snapped, hands on her waist. "Those dead people were our friends!"

"I know, I know," Josh replied, raising both hands and taking a step back. "I didn't mean it that way. Really. I just meant . . ."

"He meant it's going to be really painful to look at the yearbook," Stacy said, lowering her eyes.

"Yes. That's what I meant," Josh replied quickly. "It—it's been such a horrible year. So many frightening deaths. So many kids . . ." His voice trailed off.

Stacy dropped onto a chair and shoved her backpack away from her. She shook her head. "Marla worked so hard on this yearbook. I—I can't believe she's dead. I can't believe she'll never get to see it. I—"

A sob escaped Stacy's throat. Josie hurried across the room and wrapped her in a hug. The two girls tried to comfort each other.

Josie didn't see Matty Winger enter the

room. She felt a tap on her shoulder.

"You can hug me, *too*, if you like," Matty said.

Josie stepped back. "Is that some kind of threat?" she cracked. She wiped tears from her eyes with her fingers.

"I heard the yearbooks are coming," Matty said. He picked up a piece of chalk and wrote MATTY RULES in big letters on the chalkboard.

"So when are you coming home?" Josh called from the doorway.

"I'll be home before dinner," Josie replied. "I have to see the yearbooks, don't I?"

Josh disappeared without answering.

"I know you can't wait to see my outstanding photos," Matty said. He raised the chalk to his mouth and bit it in half. Then he started to chew.

Josie didn't react. She had seen him do it at least a hundred times.

"That's one of the dumbest things you do," Stacy told him, rolling her eyes.

"No way," Matty replied, chewing. "I do a *lot* of dumber things!" He laughed at his own joke. He always laughed at his own jokes.

The girls just shook their heads.

"Here. Want a piece?" Matty offered a stick of chalk to Stacy. "It's from 1996. A very good year for chalk."

"You're totally disturbed," Stacy muttered.

"Is that a compliment?" Matty shot back. He spit a white, chalky glob into the wastebasket.

"Gross," Stacy muttered, turning away.

Josie sighed and wrapped her arms around herself. "Where are those year-books?" She glanced at the wall clock. It was nearly early three-thirty. "Josh is right," she murmured sadly.

"About what?" Matty asked.

"The yearbooks. They're going to be so painful to look at. I mean . . . just seeing the smiling faces of all our friends who . . . who aren't here anymore."

Stacy lowered her gaze. "You're right," she said softly. "The hardest part was putting together the special memorial section, the tribute to everyone who died. I cried that whole night."

"Me, too," Josie murmured.

"But . . . but at least it's going to look really nice," Stacy said softly. "It's a great tribute to them all, a good way to remember them."

Matty shook his head. "I couldn't write any funny photo captions this year," he griped. "It all had to be so serious. I couldn't write anything sarcastic."

Stacy raised her dark eyes to him. "You could be sarcastic about yourself, Matty," she cracked. "Nobody would care."

He grinned at her. His lips were white from chalk dust.

Insults always bounce right off him, Josie thought. You can say anything to Matty, and he'll just grin.

The yearbooks arrived a few minutes later. Two of the custodians wheeled the big cartons in on dollies and stacked them against a wall.

Matty and Josie slid a carton into the middle of the room and began to rip it open.

"Will you sign my yearbook?" Matty asked Josie. "Sign it, 'Love forever. You're the Greatest. I'll never forget you'?"

"But I *already* forgot you!" Josie replied.

"Is that a yes?" Matty demanded.

Josie pulled out a couple of yearbooks. She used her hand to dust off the cover of the top one, then handed it to Stacy. Matty grabbed a yearbook out of the box and sat down on a table to examine it in his lap.

"Mmmmm. They smell so good!" Stacy exclaimed, her nose in the pages.

"You're supposed to read it, not inhale it," Matty told her.

"I love the smell of new books," Stacy replied.

"Disturbing," Matty muttered. He pulled open the heavy cover and gazed at the title page. "*The Beacon*. Whoever thought of that name? I don't even know what a beacon is. Is it something you have with eggs in the morning?"

"Ha ha," Stacy replied sarcastically. "You're so funny, I may start to laugh one of these days."

Josie squeezed the book in her lap. She hadn't opened it yet. She realized she was holding her breath. She squeezed the heavy covers until her hands ached.

I can't open this, she thought.

It's too sad. It's all too sad.

But I have to. It's my senior yearbook, after all. All the memories—good and bad— of my last year at Shadyside High.

Josie let her breath out in a long whoosh. Then, her heart pounding, she opened the book.

I'll look at the special memorial section first, she decided. I'll get it out of the way. Then I can check out the rest of the book.

The memorial section wasn't hard to find. It was in the front, and the pages all had heavy black borders.

So many dead friends, she thought, holding her breath again. But we used the nicest photos of them. At least I'll always be able to remember them when they were young . . . and happy.

The black-bordered pages fell open.

Josie gazed down at them.

Gary Fresno . . . Deirdre Palmer . . . Ty Sullivan . . . Debra Lake . . . Marla . . .

Marla . . .

"Nooooooo!" Josie's horrified scream echoed off the wall of classroom windows.

The photos. The beautiful photos. They had all changed!

No faces of her friends. No happy, smiling faces.

Hideous, ghoulish skulls stared up from the pages at her.

Corpses. Decaying corpses.

How did this happen? *How?*

Josie frantically flipped through the pages. All of the photos. All of them . . .

Faces from the grave.

Pock-marked skulls with rotting chunks of skin and sunken, staring . . . accusing eyes.

Chapter Two

Party Time

"We can't pass out these yearbooks," Stacy murmured. "Something happened. Something horrible."

Matty stared down at the book in his lap in stunned silence. His face was suddenly as pale as the chalk he'd been chewing.

For once, even Matty can't speak, Josie thought. Cold dread sent chill after chill down her back.

She slammed the yearbook shut. When it fell to the floor, she made no attempt to pick it up.

"All that work *wasted*!" Stacy cried. "How did this happen? Who switched the photos? Who would *do* such a horrible thing?"

I can't think about it now, Josie told herself.

I don't *want* to think about it.

She shut her eyes and saw the hideous skulls again, grinning out at her from their black-bordered pages.

"No!" she gasped. "It's enough. Haven't we suffered enough?"

Before Josie even realized it, she was on her feet, moving quickly to the door.

She heard Stacy and Matty calling to her. But she didn't stop to reply or explain.

She hurried past the cartons of yearbooks. Pushed herself out the doorway. Burst into the hall, empty except for a few cheerleaders coming from practice. A few other kids lingered by the front door.

Where am I going? Josie asked herself. What am I doing?

I can't go home. I'll just sit in my room and see those ugly photos again and again.

But where can I go? Where can I go where I *won't* see them?

My friends . . . good friends . . . their skin rotted away . . . their eyeballs sunken in their sockets . . .

A hand grabbed Josie's shoulder, startling her from her unhappy thoughts. She spun around with a gasp—and stared into Dana Palmer's troubled face.

Dana's normally perfect hair was disheveled, falling in tangles over her eyes. Her cheeks were red and puffy. Her eyes were red-rimmed and looked as if she had been crying.

"Josie—I wanted to talk to you," Dana

said, still gripping Josie's shoulder.

"Not now," Josie choked out. "I've just had a shock. I don't really—"

"It's about the party at your house," Dana interrupted, finally lowering her hand. She clasped her hands together tensely in front of her. "The graduation party. I don't think I can come."

"Huh?" Josie gaped at her.

"Thanks for inviting me," Dana said, avoiding Josie's gaze. "But with my sister gone . . . with Deirdre gone . . ." The words caught in her throat. Shiny tears rolled down her cheeks.

Josie stared at her, wishing she could say something to comfort Dana. But what could she do? Deirdre had died during Spring Break in Tucson—on a trip that Dana was supposed to take.

Dana had acted so strangely ever since. Sometimes so sad, she refused to speak to anyone. Sometimes too cheerful, so that everyone knew she was playacting.

Dana's moods shot up and down like a roller-coaster ride.

At the prom, Josie remembered, Dana had acted totally giddy, clinging to Mickey Myers, appearing so happy.

But now she gazed at Josie, pale and shaken. "I don't think I can come to your party," Dana whispered. And then her voice filled with emotion. "I miss her so much! So much!"

"I—I miss her, *too*," Josie stammered. "I

miss Deirdre every day."

Deirdre had been Josie's closest friend. Josie had never been that close with Dana. But she hugged her now.

The two girls hugged each other and felt each other's teardrops against their burning cheeks.

"You should try to come, Dana," Josie said finally, wiping her wet cheeks with both hands. "We all feel the same way. We all have lost someone this year. But please try to come to the party."

Dana sighed and pushed wet tangles of blond hair off her face.

"Josh and I know that no one is in a party mood," Josie continued. "We don't feel like celebrating, either. But I just think we should all be together for one last time. It—it's the last chance we'll have before we all go our separate ways."

She waited for Dana to reply. But Dana stared at her, breathing hard, her cheeks red and tear-stained. "See you," Dana murmured finally. She turned and ran off, her shoes thudding hard on the hallway floor.

Josie watched until Dana disappeared around a corner. Then she slumped against a locker and shut her eyes.

Maybe the idea of a graduation party *is* crazy, she thought. Maybe we should just graduate and try to forget this year ever happened.

Pressing her back against the cool metal

of the locker, Josie tried to clear her mind. She didn't want to think about the yearbook photos . . . or about her senior year.

She didn't want to think about the party where the horror had all begun.

But she couldn't stop the memories from sweeping through her mind, rushing over her like a tidal wave of ugliness, of death.

It seemed like a hundred years ago—last June, the first party of the summer, their first party as seniors. Trisha Conrad had the party at her family's beautiful mansion overlooking the river.

What a great time they were having—until the intruder arrived.

The intruder in the long, flowing red cloak and hood.

Josie could see it all so clearly. The French doors bursting open. The cloaked figure floating into the house.

The hood falling back, revealing a rotting skull, gleaming yellow under the bright ceiling lights. Empty eye sockets like deep caverns. And in place of eyes—two hissing snake heads wriggling out from the dark sockets.

Once again, for the thousandth time, Josie saw the skull's jaws creak open. And heard the dry wheeze of ugly laughter escape. "*Heeee . . . heee . . . heeee.*"

It was an evil spirit, Josie knew.

She knew because she had summoned it.

My fault, Josie realized. All my fault.

The red-cloaked spirit killed Gary Fresno first. It heaved him into the wall so hard, his head made a sick splattering sound—and the whole wall cracked apart.

The evil creature tore off Trisha's ear, ripped away her scalp. Tore her to pieces. Then it shoved its bony fist straight through Marla Newman's body.

Josie watched it kill them. She watched it kill them all.

Even Josh. Even Josh.

All dead. The whole senior class—except for Josie.

Josie escaped. She knew she was the only one who could defeat the evil spirit.

Because she had summoned it.

Why? Why did she chant the ancient spell in the tiny library in Jennifer Fear's house? If only she had known the evil she would unleash.

And now they were all dead. All of her friends. She had watched the evil spirit murder them all.

Was there anything she could do to stop the evil?

Josie hurried to Jennifer's house. She hurried there to conjure another spell. A spell to turn time back. To bring them all back. To send the evil spirit away.

She had succeeded—and she had failed.

She turned time back one hour. She brought everyone back to life.

None of the seniors realized what had happened.

None of them remembered the scene of horror. Because to them, it had never happened.

Josie was so happy, so joyful and excited, she wanted to hug each one of them.

But her happiness didn't last long. She had succeeded—but she had also failed.

The spirit did not vanish. Its evil stayed on.

How else could you explain the horrors of senior year? The tragic deaths? The terrifying accidents?

Each death of a classmate plunged Josie deeper into a pit of guilt. Is it all my fault? she wondered. Is the evil spirit I unleashed responsible for all the horror?

She prayed that the spirit was gone. She prayed that it had completed its evil work.

But the ugly yearbook photos . . . the frightening nightmare about the bleeding graduation robes . . .

Were they a sign?

A sign that the spirit was still near? That it was waiting for graduation? Waiting to kill them all?

Josie shuddered.

She opened her eyes and took an unsteady step away from the locker.

And then she stopped as a dark shadow swept over her.

"It's *you*!" Josie murmured.

Chapter Three

Trisha Bleeds

"**Y**ou—Matty!" Josie narrowed her eyes at Matty Winger. "Why did you sneak up on me like that?"

Matty shrugged. "I didn't mean to." He studied her face. "Your eyes were closed. What were you doing?"

"Uh . . . just thinking about things," Josie replied. No way she could tell Matty what was troubling her. He'd just make a dumb joke and laugh.

"Look at this," Matty said, lowering his gaze. He held an open yearbook in his hands. "You won't believe this."

"Oh no," Josie groaned. "Something else?"

Had *all* the photos changed into decaying skulls?

Matty stabbed a chubby finger at a square on the page. "This is too weird," he said.

Josie gazed at the gray square. "What's wrong?"

"It's supposed to be Clark Dickson's senior photo," Matty explained. "But it's a blank square."

"So? Big deal. The printer just made a mistake," Josie replied impatiently.

"That's what I thought," Matty said. He slammed the book shut. "But I went back and looked at the film."

"And?"

"I took half a roll of Clark. I checked all the negatives. Blank. Every one of them is blank."

Josie frowned. "So you think—"

"We all call him Count Clarkula," Matty interrupted excitedly. "We all joke that he's a vampire because he dresses in black and acts so weird. But it's no joke! He really *is* a vampire! This proves it!"

Josie rolled her eyes. "Or it proves that you're a rotten photographer!"

Matty argued with her a while longer. But Josie barely listened. She didn't want to think about Clark being a vampire. She didn't want to think about *anything*. Her brain felt ready to explode!

She hurried to her locker.

Matty followed close behind, slapping the yearbook with one hand, begging her to listen to him. Josie pulled open her locker and loaded books into her backpack.

"We have a vampire in the school, and you're just ignoring it," Matty moaned. "We have to tell someone. We have real proof here. We have to *do* something."

He was standing right on top of her. Josie shoved him back with both hands. "I have an idea. Why don't you go over to Clark's house and drive a stake through his heart?"

"Ha ha. Very funny," he muttered.

"I—I've got to go," Josie stammered.

She didn't wait for his reply. She turned and ran out of the building.

In front of her house, she found Josh washing his car. When he saw her, he raised the garden hose and sent a spray of water in her direction.

"Did the yearbooks come?" he called. "Did you bring one home?"

"They have to go back," Josie told him, shaking her head.

"Huh? What do you mean?"

"I mean there was . . . a mistake. Some pages are messed up."

She didn't feel like describing it to him. "A printer's mistake, I guess," she lied.

"You mean we don't get our yearbooks before school is over?" Josh demanded.

"Boo-hoo, Josh," Josie said sarcastically. "Think you'll survive?"

Josh sighed. "What a messed-up year."

"Maybe we should cancel the graduation party," Josie blurted out.

"No way," Josh replied quickly. "We have to have *some* fun this year. Why should we cancel it?"

"Well, Dana came up to me after school.

She said she's too sad and upset to celebrate. And other kids—"

"That's why we *have* to do the party!" Josh
insisted. "Of course we don't feel like celebrating. But we can't just wallow in unhappi-
ness. We can't spend the rest of our lives
thinking about what a tragic, horrible year
we had. We can't let it *defeat* us!"

"Okay, okay. Calm down," Josie said softly.
She watched the neighbor's beagle sniff a
tree. It started to rub its back against the
rough bark of the trunk.

Dogs have it easy, Josie thought.

She made her way into the house. Maybe
I'm wrong about graduation, she thought.
Maybe we'll all be okay.

She tried not to think about anything that
night.

But the next morning a piercing scream
brought the horror back to her.

Josie had just arrived at school. The first bell
had already rung. She bent to pick up some
notebooks from the bottom of her locker.

The high, shrill scream made Josie leap to
her feet. Her books scattered over the floor.

She spun around to see Trisha Conrad at
the other end of the hall.

Did Trisha scream?

Who was that behind her?

Clark?

Count Clarkula?

Jumping over her books, Josie took off,
running to Trisha.

She was halfway down the hall when Trisha screamed again.

And Josie saw the blood.

"Trisha!" Josie shrieked. "Trisha—!"

Why was Trisha covered in blood?

Chapter Four

"We're Not Going to Graduate!"

"Trisha—what happened?" Josie called breathlessly.

Clark stepped up beside Trisha. "She—she cut her arm!" he cried.

Her heart pounding, Josie stopped in front of them. Blood poured from Trisha's wrist, onto her jeans, onto the floor.

"I don't believe it! It's really bleeding!" Trisha cried. "Stupid display case!"

Josie turned and gazed at the glass case on the wall. "What were you doing?" she asked Trisha.

"Arranging the stupid trophies," Trisha groaned. "I—I didn't see that broken piece of glass."

"It's a pretty deep cut," Josie said. "We need to wrap something around it to stop the flow—"

She stopped when she saw Clark's eyes

close. He started to sway.

"Clark—what's wrong?" Josie demanded.

"Sorry," he replied unsteadily. He grabbed the wall to steady himself. "It's the blood. I never could stand the sight of blood. Ooh—I'm a little dizzy."

Josie stared hard at him. Count Clarkula? Can't stand the sight of blood?

"Let's get Trisha to the nurse," Josie instructed, still studying Clark.

"Ow. It hurts!" Trisha wailed. "Of all the stupid things!"

Josie and Clark each took an arm. Luckily, the nurse's office was right around the corner.

Ms. Kramer jumped up from her desk as soon as they entered. She was a young woman with curly black hair and wire-rimmed glasses perched on a slender nose.

"My wrist—" Trisha moaned. "I cut it on the glass display case."

Ms. Kramer took the arm tenderly and raised it to her face to examine it. "Pretty deep cut," she murmured. "But I don't think you'll need stitches."

Trisha sighed with relief.

"Let's get it cleaned up, and I'll wrap it for you," the nurse said. She led Trisha to the back office.

"I'd better get to class," Clark called. He still appeared pale and shaken. "See you later, Trisha." He disappeared down the hall.

Huh? *Later?* Josie thought.

Later?

Why would Trisha be seeing Count Clarkula later?

Trisha had been seeing Gary Fresno all year. When Gary was killed, Trisha took it very hard. She didn't come to school for a week. Every time Josie phoned to see how she was, Trisha began crying too hard to talk.

So she can't be seeing Clark, Josie thought. That would be just too weird.

She waited for the nurse to finish bandaging Trisha's wrist. Then she walked with Trisha down the empty hall toward their physics class.

"Just a few more days," Trisha murmured.

"Excuse me?"

"Just a few more days, and we're outta here!" Trisha sent her straight blond hair back with a toss of her head. She spoke through gritted teeth, a strange, unpleasant smile on her mouth.

"Look at me. I'm covered with blood. We're all covered with blood," she said bitterly. Her voice sounded hollow in the long, empty hall. "I never want to see this place again."

"It's such a shame," Josie murmured. "It was supposed to be a special year. It—"

She stopped when she saw Trisha grab the wall. "Hey—what's wrong?"

Trisha's knees collapsed. She sank to the floor. Her eyes rolled up in her head until

Josie could see only the whites.

A frightening moan escaped Trisha's throat. On her knees on the floor, her whole body shook.

It lasted only a second.

Before Josie could react, Trisha revived. She squinted up at Josie as if she didn't recognize her. Then she shook her head hard, her blond hair falling over her face.

"Wow," Trisha murmured. "Wow."

Josie helped her to her feet. "Trisha—"

"I just saw something," Trisha said in a whisper. "Another one of my visions."

She shut her eyes and leaned against the tile wall. "It was so horrible, Josie. I—I don't want to talk about it."

Another vision, Josie realized. That was Trisha's power as a Fear descendant. She was having another psychic flash.

"What did you see?" Josie urged, her heart suddenly racing. "Tell me. I really want to know."

Eyes still closed, Trisha shuddered. "I saw the auditorium. All decked out for graduation. The chairs all lined up on the stage. Banners on the wall. A podium. But . . . but . . ."

"But—what?" Josie demanded.

"No one there," Trisha continued, opening her eyes wide in horror, seeing it again. "No one in the auditorium. Only row after row of . . . coffins."

Josie gasped. She grabbed Trisha's arm. "Oh, no," she murmured.

"Yes, coffins," Trisha whispered, nodding. "The coffins were open. I saw a dead body in every coffin. The corpses all wore caps and gowns. Red caps and gowns."

This is like my dream, Josie thought.

Trisha turned to her. Tears shimmered in her eyes. Her chin trembled.

She grabbed Josie's shoulders with both hands. "Don't you see?" Trisha cried. "Don't you see what it means?"

"Yes," Josie started. "Yes, I—"

"We're not going to graduate!" Trisha cried. "Whatever it is that has doomed our class—*it's not going to let us graduate!*"

PART TWO

Chapter Five

"I'm Not a Vampire!"

Clark pulled the black Mustang into a parking space in front of the mall entrance, then cut the engine and the lights. He climbed out of the car, stretched and sighed, brushing his black hair straight back.

He didn't like shopping, especially for clothes. It was too hard to know what would look right on him. He always felt too tall, too thin and gawky in clothing stores. He had such pale skin. Some colors made him look even paler.

That's why I always wear black, he told himself, strolling toward the mall entrance, both hands in the pockets of his black denims. It cuts down on the choices.

But maybe I'll surprise everyone at the graduation party, he thought, a thin smile spreading over his face, dark eyes glimmering. Show up in purple. Or blue.

He stopped in front of a store window and gazed at a silky, bright red polo shirt.

Oooh—not red.

The color reminded him of the blood—Trisha's blood. He pictured Trisha cutting her wrist that morning. The blood draining out, splashing on the floor.

No.

Stop thinking about it, he ordered himself.

It had made him so dizzy. Even Josie had seen how sick it made him.

He spun away from the window, the bright white light lingering in his eyes. He stepped past a woman with a double stroller, two babies bawling their heads off, shaking tiny fists. Sweeping his hair back again, Clark entered the mall.

He made his way past the bubbling fountain in front, past the open entrance to Dalby's Department Store. Too expensive for him.

Humming to himself, he strolled past two or three shoe stores, a bookstore with a table out front stacked high with paperbacks.

Were those kids hanging out at the door to the Greasy Spoon from Shadyside High? He didn't recognize them.

Across the aisle he saw a row of clothing stores. Dudes & Dudettes. No way. He hated all that surfer stuff. Eddie's. Yeah. Eddie's. Not a bad place. A lot of kids bought stuff there. He could probably find something not too expensive, not too tacky.

He stepped into the store. Blue spotlights. Jimi Hendrix booming out of the music system. Shelves of jeans. Some funky shirts.

And Matty Winger.

Huh? Matty Winger?

"Hey, yo—Clark!" Matty was just as surprised to see Clark.

"How's it going?" Clark muttered. He turned back to the entrance as if seeking an escape route.

"Check out this vest," Matty said, a grin on his chubby face, a mustard stain on his chin. "It's suede or something."

"Looks more like 'or something,'" Clark joked.

Matty looked hurt. "It's kind of like a cowboy thing, don't you think?"

"Whatever," Clark shrugged.

"*Foxy lady . . . foxy lady*," Jimi Hendrix sang.

Clark realized that Matty was staring at him. The blue lights gave Matty's skin a ghostly glow. "What's your problem?" Clark demanded.

"Your yearbook photo," Matty said.

Clark wasn't sure he heard right. "Excuse me?"

"Your yearbook photo—it didn't come out," Matty said, stammering, nervous.

"Of course not," Clark sneered. "You took it—remember?"

Matty didn't laugh. "No. I mean, the whole

35

roll. The negatives were all blank."

"So?" Clark narrowed his eyes at Matty. *What is he thinking? What is he trying to say? The poor guy is so tense, he's practically shaking.*

"I told you it was too dark in that room," he told Matty. "Remember? You weren't sure about the shutter speed. You said you'd never used that camera before."

Matty stared back at him silently.

"Okay, okay, I know what you're thinking!" Clark exclaimed. "You think I'm a vampire because my photos didn't turn out, and vampires can't be photographed."

Matty gasped, shocked by Clark's honesty. "Well . . . no. I mean, I—"

"I know all the rumors about me," Clark sneered, shaking his head. "I know they call me Count Clarkula." He grinned. "I like it."

Matty's mouth dropped open. "You *do*?"

Clark nodded. "Sure. At least kids notice me. At least kids are talking about me."

"Well . . . yeah," Matty admitted uncomfortably. "But you don't mind—?"

"They think I'm a bad dude," Clark said, snickering. "It's dumb, but I like having a bad image. Why do you think I dress in black?"

"I guess—"

"Girls think I'm interesting," Clark confided, lowering his voice. "They think I'm dangerous. So why should I set them straight? Why not go along with it?"

Matty nodded solemnly. "I see."

Clark was enjoying this conversation. He could see Matty's brain spinning. He knew that Matty never expected him to confide in him this way.

He and Matty had never been friends. This was the first real conversation they'd ever had.

"Guess who is going out with me tomorrow night?" Clark asked, his dark eyes reflecting the blue store light.

"Wh-who?" Matty stammered, crinkling the suede vest between his hands.

"Trisha Conrad," Clark revealed. He enjoyed Matty's gasp of surprise.

"She's going out with *you*?"

Clark chuckled. "You really think I'm a vampire—don't you!" he accused.

Matty took a step back. His expression changed. "No. I—"

"I'm not a vampire," Clark said slowly, softly, his eyes locked on Matty's. "I can prove it."

"That's okay," Matty said, taking another step back, stumbling over a rack of khakis. "I'll take your word for it, Clark. Really."

"No. Come over," Clark insisted. "I really want to prove it to you. Enough of these stupid rumors. Come over to my house. Right now. I'll show you."

Matty stared at him suspiciously. "You mean you'll show me photographs of you?"

Clark put a hand on Matty's beefy shoulder. He started to guide him out of the store.

"I'll prove to you that I'm not a vampire. Come on."

Matty pulled back. Clark glimpsed a flash of fear on his face.

"Come on," Clark urged.

Matty studied him. Studied him, thinking hard. Then he shrugged. "Okay. Let's go."

Chapter Six

"Stop Kidding Around, Clark"

They drove along Division Street in Clark's Mustang. Clark kept his eyes on the traffic and didn't say much. Whenever he glanced at the passenger seat, he caught a tense expression on Matty's face.

Matty cranked the radio up and kept pushing the buttons, changing rapidly from station to station. He wiped sweat off his forehead with the back of his hand.

Clark turned his face away so that Matty wouldn't catch him laughing. *He's scared to death!* Clark thought. And he isn't doing a very good job of hiding it.

Poor Matty.

He's a total geek. But you have to feel sorry for the guy.

Clark pulled the car up the gravel driveway to the back of the house. He pushed open the car door and climbed out, stretching his arms over his head.

It was a cool, moonless night. A sharp breeze made the old trees in the backyard creak and groan. The house stood dark except for a single pale bulb over the back stoop.

Clark pushed open the kitchen door, clicked on the light, and motioned for Matty to follow him into the house.

"No one home?" Matty murmured, lingering by the side of the car.

"Guess they went out," Clark replied softly, enjoying Matty's fear.

"How are you going to prove you're not a vampire?" Matty asked, still not moving toward the house.

A cat cried somewhere down the block. A sharp gust of wind sent a metal trash can lid clattering onto the driveway.

Clark snickered. "I'm not a vampire. I'm a werewolf!"

Matty let out a weak laugh. "Very funny. Remind me to laugh later."

Clark motioned for Matty to come inside. "Come on. Stop looking so terrified. When I bite your neck, it won't hurt a bit."

"You should do a stand-up act," Matty replied. "You're just a riot," he added sarcastically. He followed Clark into the kitchen.

Matty gazed around nervously. "Did you hear the one about the vampire that goes into a blood bank?" he asked, his voice tight, his forehead beaded with sweat.

"I've heard all your jokes," Clark said. He guided Matty to the stairs, turning on lights along the way. The house felt warm despite the cool air outside. Clark noticed that all the windows were closed.

Matty was breathing hard when they reached the second-floor landing.

"You're out of shape," Clark told him. "Do you run or work out or anything?"

"No. I might go to a gym this summer," Matty replied. "Do you work out?"

Clark shook his head. "No. I just flap my bat wings and fly. It's really good exercise."

Matty uttered a nervous laugh.

Clark stepped aside and let Matty go into his room first. Then Clark clicked on the ceiling light.

His bed was made, but the room was cluttered and messy. A pair of black denims was tossed on the floor beside the bed. A few of Clark's black shirts were crumpled in a ball on the desk chair. Books and magazines were strewn everywhere.

"Nice room," Matty muttered, gazing around.

Clark closed the door and clicked the lock.

"Hey—what's the big idea?" Matty demanded.

Clark ignored him.

He motioned for Matty to sit down. "Just move that stuff away."

Matty hesitated. "Uh . . . that's okay. I can only stay a minute. Got to get home. What's your proof? What did you want to show me?"

His cheeks were suddenly pink, full of blood. Clark could see a vein throbbing in Matty's neck.

Clark moved closer, his arms folded in front of him. "Trisha cut her wrist on a display case in school today," he began.

Matty's eyes widened. He swallowed. "Really? Is she okay?"

Clark didn't answer. His eyes locked on Matty's. "The blood flowed," Clark said. "All red and ripe and warm and delicious."

Matty opened his mouth in a forced laugh. "Ha ha. Stop kidding around, Clark. That isn't funny."

"I know it isn't funny," Clark replied, lowering his voice to a whisper. "I wanted to grab her arm, bring her wrist to my mouth, and drink. Lap it up . . . Drink it all down while it was still so fresh."

Matty's eyes grew even wider. His round cheeks darkened to red. He took a step back, stumbling over a pair of black hightop sneakers.

"You—you're kidding, right?" Matty stammered.

Clark stepped closer. "What do *you* think, Matty? Do you think I'm kidding?" he demanded coldly.

Matty nodded, sweat flying off his forehead. Clark could see that he was breathing hard.

"I know what you're doing," Matty said. "You're just trying to scare me so you can tell everyone at school how stupid I am."

"Is *that* what I'm doing?" Clark asked, not blinking, holding his steady stare on the other boy's frightened face.

Matty swallowed again. "Look, I'm sorry," he said. "I know I was totally stupid. I know you're not a vampire. All that Count Clarkula stuff is totally dumb. I'll tell everyone."

He started to the door.

Clark blocked his path.

"But it's not dumb, Matty," he said, bringing his face close to the other boy's. "Don't you see? I'm confessing to you."

"Huh? You're *what*?"

"I'm confessing to you," Clark repeated. "You're the first person I've told. I really am a vampire."

"No. Come on," Matty uttered. He had his eyes on the door. "This isn't funny. I learned my lesson—okay? I know all the rumors must have hurt your feelings. I know—"

"But the rumors are *true*!" Clark insisted, raising his voice to a shout. "The kids at school are right about me. I'd never confess it. I'd never tell you. But seeing all that blood from Trisha's wrist . . . it . . . it made me so *thirsty*!"

"Cut it out!" Matty cried. "This is crazy!"

Clark leaned over him. "It made me so thirsty," he repeated softly. "And then you came along at the mall. There you were, so filled with blood. Look at it . . . Look at it bursting in your cheeks, *throbbing* in your neck."

"I'm outta here!" Matty cried. "This isn't funny. You're *sick!*"

He dived toward the door.

Clark moved quickly, stepping in front of him, grabbing Matty's broad shoulders.

"Stop it!" Matty shrieked. "Let go! What— what are you going to do?"

Clark realized that he was breathing hard, *too*. His lips tingled, tingled with excitement. His throat felt so dry, dry as cobwebs.

He could feel Matty's shoulders tremble beneath his grip. "First I'm going to cloud your mind," he told him. "You'll never remember this. You'll never even remember that you were here."

"No—!" Matty protested, unable to hide his terror. "No—please—!"

Clark ignored Matty's pleas. "Then I'm going to satisfy my thirst," he said softly. He licked his caked, dry lips. "I'm so thirsty. So thirsty . . ."

He held Matty firmly in place. The other boy struggled weakly. But Clark had the strength of two hundred years of immortality inside him.

Matty made a gasping, wheezing sound with each breath.

Clark gazed hard into his eyes. Gazed deep into the dark circles.

He felt Matty's shoulders relax. Heard his breathing soften. Steady . . . steady . . .

Matty's eyes fluttered shut as he fell into a trance.

Steady . . . Steady.

Clark's tongue slid over his dry lips as his fangs slid down. He licked the curled yellow fangs as they slid down to his chin.

Steady . . . steady . . . But I'm so thirsty.

Saliva poured from Clark's open mouth, plopping wetly onto his shoes, onto the floor. Saliva glistened on the twin fangs as Clark opened his mouth wide.

"*Unh unh unh.*" Hungry grunts escaped his throat.

He grabbed Matty's fleshy, soft arm. He raised it to his drooling mouth.

"*Unh unh unh.*"

Clark dug his fangs deep into the soft skin at the inside of Matty's elbow.

And drank.

Sucking, slurping.

Blood and saliva mixing together.

He drank noisily, sloppily . . . hungrily.

So warm . . . so rich . . . so delicious . . .

His tongue lapped at the soft skin. Blood rolled down the arm. Plinked onto the floor.

He was still drinking when the phone rang.

"*Unh unh unh.*"

He let it ring twice. Three times.

So thirsty . . . so thirsty . . .

Who could be calling?

The ringing made his head throb.

He raised his head. Let the fangs slide out from Matty's soft flesh.

"Unh unh unh."

He let go of Matty. Watched him slump to his knees on the floor. Blood trickling down his arm from the twin puncture wounds. His eyes still closed.

Clark lurched to the bed table. Lifted the phone to his ear. "Hello?" he uttered breathlessly, the taste of the dark liquid lingering on his tongue.

"Clark? It's me."

"Oh, hi, Trisha," Clark replied. "I was just thinking about you!"

PART THREE

Chapter Seven

A Bad Hair Day

"Jennifer—you can't skip graduation rehearsal," Josie scolded into the phone. "I mean, you don't want to walk left when everyone else walks right, do you?"

She could hear her friend laughing on the other end of the line.

Josie laughed, *too*. The idea of a one-hour rehearsal was totally dumb. After all, what was there to rehearse?

"You have to practice taking the diploma with your left hand and shaking hands with your right hand," Jennifer said. "If you do it wrong, you don't graduate!"

They both laughed.

"And you have to practice balancing the cap on your head."

"And keeping the tassel from falling in your eyes!"

49

It wasn't that funny. But Josie was feeling giddy. She had been staring at her calculus workbook for over an hour—and *anything* would make her laugh!

"I've got to get back to work," she told Jennifer, tapping the eraser of her pencil against her forehead. "I have to ace the final."

"Why?" Jennifer demanded. "We'll be out of there in a few days, Josie. You're already accepted at college. Why are you working so hard on your finals? Who cares?"

"My dad cares," Josie replied with a groan. She stopped tapping the pencil and set it down on her desk. "Actually, it's not all bad. Dad says if I keep my grade average up, I might be able to get my own car."

"Might?" Jennifer asked. "Did he say *might*? Or did he say you *could* have your own car?"

Josie laughed. "*Might* is a step in the right direction. So I can't let calculus mess the whole thing up."

"Is Josh worrying about finals, *too*?" Jennifer asked.

"Josh worrying? Get serious," Josie groaned. "He's breezing through as always. Straight A's . . . Early acceptance at Penn State. Josh never has to worry."

They chatted for a few more minutes. Josie kept glancing at her bedside table clock and then back at her calculus workbook.

Finally she said good-bye to Jennifer and returned to her studying.

She could hear music blaring in Josh's room. He's so inconsiderate, she thought, frowning. How am I supposed to concentrate? She got up and closed her bedroom door.

Then she returned to her desk, leaning over the workbook, staring into the bright yellow cone of light from the desklamp, staring at the numbers on the page.

Her eyelids were beginning to feel heavy when she heard a scraping sound.

A dry cough.

"Huh?" Had she dozed off?

Josie realized she wasn't alone. "Josh?"

No.

A moan of horror escaped her throat as she raised her eyes to the hooded figure in the red cloak.

"Noooooo!"

Am I dreaming?

The bedroom window was closed. But the cloak rustled and shimmered as if blown by a strong breeze.

Another dry cough—and then the hood fell back.

And the yellow skull was revealed, powdery and cracked. Empty eye sockets so deep and dark. Teeth cracked and rotting.

"*Hee hee heeeee.*"

A laugh as dry as wind, a laugh like crackling dead leaves.

Am I dreaming? Josie wondered, gaping in horror from behind the desk. Unable to stand. Unable to move.

Her hands suddenly seemed so cold. Cold as a corpse?

She could feel the blood throbbing at her temples.

The broken-toothed grin. The empty eye sockets trained on her as if they could see.

"*I'm . . . back . . .*" The words escaping the open jaw in a hoarse, ugly rasp.

The red cloak fluttering, fluttering, even though there was no breeze.

No air.

No air to breathe.

Josie felt herself choking. Felt her temples throb. Felt her heart pound.

No. I'm dreaming again.

Wake up, Josie. Wake up.

But the grinning figure fluttered in front of her, shimmering, so ugly, so evil. "*I'm . . . back. I'm . . . not . . . finished.*"

"Noooo!" Josie screamed. "You murdered so many of my friends! Go away! Go *away!*"

The yellow skull pulled back into the shadow of the hood. The black, empty eyeholes stared at her. Deep inside them, Josie could see the two snake heads, tongues darting in and out, jaws snapping.

"Go away—please!" Josie begged. "This is just a dream. Just a dream!"

The twin snakes unfurled from the eye sockets of the skull, stretched . . . stretched as if reaching for Josie.

"*Not a dream . . .*" the evil spirit croaked. "*I'll show you.*"

The long cloak fluttered. The skull sank into the scarlet hood.

And as Josie stared in horror, the figure began to fade. Slowly . . . so slowly . . . shimmering darker, darker, like a fire slowly dying.

Josie stared across her room. Her hands still cold and wet. Her temples still throbbing.

She shut her eyes. Blinked a few times, making sure the figure was really gone.

"*I'll show you*," it had rasped.

What did that mean?

"*I'll show you*."

Her whole body trembling, Josie started to pull herself to her feet. But she sank back down in her chair when her head started to tingle.

Tingle and itch.

"Ohhh." What's going on? she wondered.

The itching circled her whole scalp, grew intense.

At first it tickled. Then it burned.

"My hair—"

Chills rolled down her back. Her whole head itched. Her hair tingled, tingled so hard it *hurt*.

She reached a hand up and started to scratch.

Scratching didn't help.

"Oh!"

She scratched harder.

Felt something warm and soft under her fingernails.

Another one. Another one.

What is crawling in my head?

She squirmed and thrashed.

I can't take it! The itching—it's driving me crazy!

She scraped her fingers frantically over her scalp.

Pulled something out, something small, and white, and wriggling.

"Oh, no . . ."

A maggot.

Josie screamed. She dug her fingers into her hair. Desperately scraped them across her scalp.

Maggots fell to the desktop. Maggots crawled over her fingers, over her hands.

"Help me—somebody! Help me!"

Her hair, her head—covered with maggots. Hundreds of maggots, crawling over her . . . crawling, crawling . . .

Chapter Eight

Josie Totally Freaks

She shampooed her hair again and again. At least seven times, scrubbing with both hands, watching the white worms rain into the drain.

Sobbing and shuddering, chill after chill racking her body, she scrubbed the maggots out. But she knew that a *hundred* shampoos wouldn't erase the tingling of her scalp—or the picture of the disgusting maggots wriggling through her hair.

"I'll never forget this," Josie sobbed.

She used two bath towels to dry her hair. Rubbed so hard. Brushed her hair out, squinting into the steamy mirror, searching for more of the tiny, white worms.

Yes! They were gone! Down the drain.

Still shivering, Josie wrapped a towel tightly around her hair. Tight enough to keep them from returning?

No. The evil spirit had sent them. Sent them as a sign. As a sign that he wasn't a dream. That he was still there. That his work wasn't finished.

"What am I going to do?" Josie asked her reflection in the bathroom mirror. "I can't fight this on my own. I have to get help."

She pulled on jeans and a maroon and white Shadyside High sweatshirt. The phone rang.

The sound made her jump. She stared at the phone, letting it ring. Her hair tingled beneath the tightly wrapped towel.

Finally she picked up the phone. "Hello?"

She heard a familiar voice on the other end. Phoebe Yamura. "Josie, I just got home from the Cheerleader Awards ceremony at school. I need help with calculus. Can I go over some problems with you?"

Josie heard the words clearly, but she couldn't get them to make sense. She pictured the maggots pouring into the shower drain like grains of rice.

"I—I can't right now, Phoebe," she replied shakily.

"I can call later," Phoebe said. "Just a few problems, Josie. I really need some help. You see—"

"I—I just can't!" Josie screamed. She shut off the phone and tossed it across the room.

Don't worry about it, Phoebe. None of us are going to be alive for the calculus final, she thought bitterly.

Her legs trembled as she made her way down the hall to Josh's room. The door was closed. Music blared from the other side.

She had to knock three times. Finally Josh opened the door. He wore an enormous white T-shirt over baggy denim shorts. His hair stood straight up. He squinted out at her through the half-open door.

"You woke me up," he groaned.

"You were sleeping with that music on?" Josie exclaimed.

He nodded. "Just taking a nap."

"I—I have to talk to you," she stammered.

"Now?" he protested. "I have to make some calls. Do some stuff. Maybe later we can—"

She pushed him out of the way and strode into the room. He had three open Coke bottles on the floor and a half-eaten bag of nacho chips. Jeans and shirts were tossed everywhere.

"Hey—I said I have to make some calls," he said sharply.

Josie ignored him. She shoved some books off the bed and dropped down on the edge. "Turn off the music," she ordered. "This is important, Josh. I—I'm so scared."

Her expression must have frightened him. He stopped arguing and turned off the stereo. Then he pulled his desk chair in front of her, turned it around, and sat on it backward. "Okay. Speak. What's your problem?"

Josie took a deep breath. "I haven't told

you any of this. I don't know where to begin."

"How about at the beginning?" Josh replied, drumming his hands on the back of the wooden chair.

"You're not going to believe me," Josie said softly.

A grin spread slowly over Josh's face. "Oh, I get it. Is it about a guy? Who is it? Someone at school?"

Josie let out a frustrated growl. "Just shut up. This is serious. Really serious," she said through gritted teeth.

"Then it *is* about a guy!"

"Shut up!" she snapped.

His grin faded. He leaned his head on his arms against the back of the chair. "Okay. Shoot."

"Just listen to the whole story," Josie pleaded. "And try to believe me." She took another deep breath. "I did a terrible thing. I didn't mean to, but I did. I called up an evil spirit."

Josh blinked. He opened his mouth to say something. But Josie's sharp stare made him stop.

Her voice trembled as she told him the whole story. It felt good to finally share it with someone, as if a terrible weight was being lifted off her.

But it was so hard to tell.

She told him about the little library in Jennifer Fear's house, filled with books on the occult and the dark arts. She described the Doom Spell she had chanted when everyone else had left the room. She called up an evil spirit. She didn't really mean to.

She described the evil spirit, the yellow skull, the horrifying figure in the red cloak and hood. Breathlessly she explained how the spirit had murdered everyone at Trisha Conrad's party—even Josh.

Josh gasped and narrowed his eyes at her, studying her intently.

What is he thinking? Josie wondered. Does he believe me? Does he believe *any* of this?

"I went back to Jennifer's house," Josie explained, returning her stepbrother's stare, her mouth suddenly as dry as cotton. "I sneaked back into the library. I found another spell. I was so frightened, Josh. I'd seen everyone murdered. *Everyone*.

"I moved time back an hour. Now everyone was alive again. No one even knew. No one knew anything bad had happened. But I knew. I knew the evil spirit was still out there.

"That's why so many horrible things have happened to our class this year," Josie continued with a sob. "I've had to live with this all year. I've had to live with this guilt."

She stared at him, not blinking, not moving. "And now . . . it's going to kill *everyone* at graduation. I need help, Josh. I need help to stop it. Or else it will kill us all."

His eyes burned into hers. He didn't reply.

She could practically see his mind whirring.

She grabbed his hands over the back of the chair. His hands were warm. Hers were ice cold.

"Do you believe me?" she demanded. "Believe me, Josh. Please believe me."

Silence. An eternity of silence.

And then Josh replied in a whisper, "Yes, I believe you. I really do."

She uttered a thankful sigh and shut her eyes, trying to hold back her emotions.

"We'll think of something," Josh said. "I know we will."

He climbed to his feet and disappeared from the room.

Josie sat with her eyes shut, hands clasped tightly in her lap. Finally I'm not alone, she thought. Finally someone believes me.

Now maybe Josh and I can go talk to Jennifer. We can persuade her to let us back into that library. We can find a spell to defeat the evil spirit. I know we can.

Maybe Trisha will help us since she is a real Fear. Maybe Trisha can use her psychic powers to help us.

Josie stood up. She pulled the towel off her head and hurried back to her room, fluffing out her hair with her hand. She brushed it in front of the dresser mirror, holding her breath, searching for any remaining maggots.

None.

She realized she felt a little better. The evil

spirit was still out there, she knew. Still watching and waiting.

At least she didn't have to deal with it alone.

Josie made her way downstairs. Hearing voices, she stopped outside the den door.

She peeked inside and saw Josh talking excitedly to her mother, gesturing with both hands. What was Josh saying?

"Josie really needs a doctor."

Josie gasped and pulled back from the doorway. Had they seen her? She pressed against the wall and listened to Josh.

"It's serious, Mom," he said. "All the deaths at school this year—I think they messed up Josie's head. I think she's totally freaked."

"What do you mean?" Mrs. Maxwell asked, her voice revealing her alarm.

"Mom, she's talking about evil spirits," Josh replied, lowering his voice. "She says she saw everyone in the class get murdered. She says it's all her fault. She's . . . she's gone crazy!"

He didn't believe me, Josie thought bitterly. He lied to me. He didn't believe any of it. He thinks I've freaked out.

Now what am I going to do?

She had stepped into the doorway without realizing it. She raised her eyes—and saw Josh and her mother staring at her.

"Josie—come in here," Mrs. Maxwell ordered. "I think we need to talk."

Chapter Nine

Back to the Fear Library

With a cry of protest, Josie spun out of the den doorway—and ran.

It was only a few short steps to the front door. Before she even realized what she was doing, she was out the door, running, running through a cool spring night.

A sliver of a moon winked down at her, low over the fresh-leaved trees. The unmowed lawns glistened wetly from a heavy night dew.

She ran all the way to Jennifer Fear's house. Pounded furiously on the front door. Pushed the bell. Her chest heaving. Her breath coming out in wheezing gasps. Her side aching.

How did I get here? she suddenly asked herself.

I didn't really look where I was running.

62

How did I cross streets? What was I thinking?

The door swung open before Josie could answer her own questions. Jennifer appeared in a square of bright light. "Josie— what on earth—?"

Petite Jennifer had her long, dark hair pulled back in a loose ponytail. She wore denim cutoffs and a sleeveless ribbed T-shirt.

"I—I—" Josie sputtered.

Jennifer held the storm door open for her. "Are you okay? Is someone chasing you?" She gazed over Josie's shoulder to the street.

"I ran all the way," Josie choked out. "I have to talk to you."

"Okay. Fine." Jennifer's dark eyes studied Josie.

"Call Trisha," Josie ordered, still struggling to catch her breath. "Please. Tell Trisha to get over here. Maybe she can help us."

Jennifer squinted at Josie. "Do we need help?"

"Yes," Josie replied solemnly. "Yes, we do."

Trisha arrived a few minutes later with a container of brownies. "You've got to try these," she insisted cheerfully, stepping into Jennifer's living room and pulling off the lid. "Mom and I just baked them. They're not from a mix."

Jennifer lifted a brownie from the container. "Still warm."

Trisha offered them to Josie. Josie shook her head. "I don't feel like eating. I have to—"

"I guess you've heard I'm going out with Clark," Trisha interrupted. She pulled a brownie from the box, shoved the box onto the coffee table, and dropped onto the couch beside Jennifer.

"You're *what*?" Jennifer cried.

"I know the whole school is talking about it," Trisha said, brushing chocolate crumbs off her chin.

"Trisha, please—" Josie begged.

"I'm going out with Clark after graduation rehearsal," Trisha announced.

Josie stared across the room at Trisha. I know what this is about, she thought. Poor Trisha. She's still wrecked, still torn up about Gary's death. She isn't interested in Clark. She just wants another guy to care about before school ends.

"I don't believe you, Trisha." Jennifer shook her head. "Just because you found out that you're a Fear—it doesn't mean you have to go out with a *vampire*!"

Trisha gasped. "Jen—you promised to keep my secret. Have you *told* people that I'm related to the Fears?"

"No—!" Jennifer insisted. Her face reddened. "Well . . . I just told Josie. No one else. I swear."

Jennifer found out that Trisha's great-grandfather, Henry Conrad, was married to Dominique Fear.

That made Trisha a Fear.

Jennifer told Josie about it over Spring Break.

Trisha glared at her for a long moment. Then her expression softened. "Well, anyway, Clark *isn't* a vampire!" she declared. "Those rumors are so stupid. Just because he's a little different, people start making up stories. Clark is *interesting*!"

"Oh, Trisha, you have the *worst* taste in guys!" Josie blurted out.

She instantly regretted it.

Trisha's face crumbled. Josie had really hurt her.

That was stupid, Josie scolded herself. I don't want to make Trisha angry. I need her. I need her on my side.

"You never really knew Gary," Trisha shot back, her voice breaking.

"I'm sorry. Really," Josie insisted. "I didn't mean—"

"Josie, why did you want to see us?" Jennifer interrupted, shifting her legs beneath her on the couch. "What did you want to tell us?"

I can't believe I'm going to tell it all again, Josie thought.

And will they react the same way as Josh? Will they both think I'm crazy, *too*?

Trisha and Jennifer leaned forward, gazing at Josie expectantly. "Are you in some kind of . . . trouble?" Trisha asked.

Josie shook her head. "No. We all are."

She crossed her legs, clasped her hands tightly together in her lap, and started the long, horrible story. "It all began right in this house," she said, catching Jennifer's surprise. "In the little library with all the scary old books."

She told it all again, watching her two friends as she talked. Trisha grew pale as she listened intently, biting her bottom lip, her eyes locked on Josie.

Jennifer kept trying to interrupt. But Josie motioned for her to keep quiet until she had finished the whole story.

"So, do you see what we have to do?" Josie concluded. "Do you see why I came running over here? We have to go back into the library. We have to find a spell—"

Trisha's mouth dropped open. "You mean you've kept this secret all year?"

Josie nodded.

"But—how could you?" Jennifer demanded. "Why didn't you—"

"I didn't know for sure that the evil spirit was still out there," Josie explained. "I hoped that it had vanished. And that all the terrible things that happened this year were just . . . bad luck."

She saw Jennifer and Trisha exchange glances.

"Do you believe me?" Josie asked, jumping to her feet, making her way to the two girls on the couch. "Please—say you believe me."

"I don't know," Trisha replied softly.

Jennifer just shook her head.

"Well, I don't care if you believe me or not!" Josie screamed, feeling herself lose control. "We have to go back into that library. We have to find a spell to defeat this evil thing!"

"No way," Jennifer replied, still shaking her head. "It's impossible, Josie. Come on. Graduation is in a few days. Let's just try to get through it without any more trouble."

"No!" Josie shrieked. "You don't understand. *It isn't going to let us graduate!*"

Both girls stared at her open-mouthed, shocked by her outburst.

Josie spun away from them. Her heart pounded. The living room went in and out of focus.

I'll do it without them, she thought.

If they won't help me, I'll do it without them.

She took off. Ran into the long hall. Past a wall of family portraits. A gold-framed oil painting of a seaside scene. Past the dining room with its long, dark wood table and crystal chandelier.

She saw Jennifer's mom at the end of the hall. "Josie—what's wrong?" Mrs. Fear called.

Josie didn't reply. She turned the corner. The library came into view.

Got to find a spell. Got to find the *right* spell.

Breathing hard, she grabbed the door

knob. Twisted it. Pulled the library door open.

She burst inside. Fumbled her hand over the wall until she found the light switch.

Josie clicked on the light. Blinking, she gazed around the little library.

And cried out in horror.

"Noooooo! Oh, no!"

Chapter Ten

Screams in the Auditorium

The books!

Josie spun around wildly, gazing at the empty wooden shelves.

"Where are all the books?" she cried, pressing her hands against her cheeks.

Mrs. Fear stepped up behind her. "Josie— what's wrong?" she asked with concern. "I heard you scream and—"

"The books!" Josie gasped. "The old spell books, the books on witchcraft and sorcery—"

"They're gone," Jennifer's mother replied calmly. "I sold them all."

"You *what*?" Josie choked out. "But—but—"

"I knew those old books upset Jennifer," Mrs. Fear explained. "So I got rid of them. I'm going to turn this room into a home office."

Josie let out a long, defeated sigh. She slumped against an empty shelf.

Now what do I do? she asked herself sadly.

Just wait for the evil spirit to return? Just wait to die?

"Are you getting an award?" Jennifer asked as they made their way into the auditorium the next afternoon.

A group of seniors blocked the doorway, laughing about something. Off to the side Josie saw Dana Palmer clinging to Mickey Myers, her arms around his neck.

Poor Dana, Josie thought. She just *hangs* on Mickey now. Ever since her twin sister died, Dana has needed Mickey so much. She shadows him everywhere. She's practically *smothering* him!

Josie caught the uncomfortable expression on Mickey's face. Is he going to let Dana down? she wondered. Is he going to break her heart?

"I don't think you heard a word I said." Jennifer's impatient words broke into Josie's thoughts.

"Huh? No. I mean—"

Jennifer laughed. "You're really a basket case these days, Josie."

Josie struggled to clear her mind. "What did you ask me, Jen?"

"I asked if you're getting an award. It *is* Senior Awards Assembly. Did you forget?" Jennifer pushed past a couple of guys and led the way down the sloping aisle of the auditorium.

"No. I won't be onstage. I'll just be

applauding from the audience," Josie replied wistfully.

"Well, I'm only winning an award for basketball," Jennifer sighed. "You know. For being MVP. It's not like I'm Kenny Klein or something, winning every academic award and scholarship known to man!"

They both turned their gaze to the stage. Kenny was already up there, in the first seat in the first row in front of the podium. Josie saw Kenny's parents in the auditorium. They both held cameras in their laps.

I didn't even tell my parents about the awards assembly, Josie thought. She wondered if Josh had mentioned it to them. Josh was winning some kind of science prize. And an honorable mention award for an essay he had written about democracy.

We're not big prizewinners in my family, Josie thought, watching Kenny up on the stage, enjoying a laugh with Mrs. Leonard, the vice principal.

Josie saw Trisha take a seat at the other end of the front row. Stacy sat down next to her and began chatting, tugging at the sleeves of her white blouse.

Josie turned to say something to Jennifer. But Jennifer was already climbing onto the stage.

Making her way down the aisle to the front seats, Josie waved to Josh. Behind him, she saw Clark and Matty sitting together, both talking at once.

Since when are Clark and Matty friends? Josie wondered.

She spotted a large white bandage on Matty's arm. Matty looked pale, as if he'd been sick.

"Seats, everyone!" Mrs. Leonard called.

A group of seniors in the back ignored her and kept talking. They were passing around a magazine, laughing about something inside it.

Josie slipped into the aisle seat in the third row.

"Seats, please!" the vice principal pleaded, popping the 'p' in *please* into the podium microphone so that it sounded like an explosion. "*P*-lease, peo*p*-le! Take your seats! I'd like to start the assembly *before* you graduate!"

Only a few kids laughed at her joke. The seniors in the back kept talking, sharing the magazine.

Josie saw Dana enter, hand-in-hand with Mickey. Dana leaned against him, whispered something in his ear, then made her way toward her place on the stage.

Mickey dropped down a few seats from Josie. He shook back his hair with a toss of his head. "Hey—how's it going?"

Josie shrugged in reply.

"Am I in the right place? Is this the *loser* section?" Mickey joked.

"We're not losers," Josie told him. "We're award-challenged."

He grinned and nodded his head. "Award-challenged. I should have put that on my college applications."

"Okay, we're going to start!" Mrs. Leonard announced, leaning into the podium microphone until it bumped her chin. "Come on, back there. Take your seats. I know it's your last few days here. You want me to have good memories of you—don't you?"

Several kids laughed. The group in the back finally broke up and found seats halfway down the auditorium.

"We're happy to have several parents of our senior award winners here today," the vice principal continued. "Their teachers and I know how proud you are—because we're proud of them, *too*."

She cleared her throat noisily, the sound blaring through the speakers. "It's been such a difficult year at Shadyside High. We're all happy to have something to celebrate today. We invite you all to a reception in the upstairs teachers' lounge after the assembly.

"Now, one final check," Mrs. Leonard said, turning toward the kids in the rows of folding chairs on the stage. She shielded her eyes from the bright stage lights. "Are all of our award winners on the stage?"

Kids onstage shuffled their feet, twisted around to see who else was up there with them.

Josie saw the vice principal's eyes stop at the empty folding chair in the first row next to Kenny. "Whose seat is that?" she asked. She returned to the podium and shuffled through some papers.

"Phoebe? Phoebe Yamura?" she called out. She turned to the audience. "Is Phoebe here today? Are her parents here?"

Silence.

Mrs. Leonard turned to a teacher at the end of the front row. "Is Phoebe absent today? Does anyone know if she's here or not?"

The teacher shrugged. Josie couldn't hear what he said.

"Too bad," Mrs. Leonard murmured, straightening her papers on the podium. "We'll have to give her all of her awards at a later date."

She raised her eyes to the enormous flag rolled up at the ceiling. "If you will all rise now," she announced, "we will lower the flag and begin our Senior Awards Assembly."

Everyone stood. The auditorium echoed with the squeak of chairs, the thud of shoes, coughs.

A tape of "The Star-Spangled Banner" roared out from the loudspeakers as the big U.S. flag began to unroll.

Josie watched it come down from the ceiling, the huge flag lowering as it unrolled.

"Ohh—!" A cry escaped her lips as she saw something unrolling with the flag.

A person?

A body!

A scream rang out behind her. Then shrieks of horror all around.

The cries and screams drowned out the music.

Josie screamed. Pressed her hands against her cheeks. And gaped. Gaped in disbelief, watching the girl's body swinging from side to side, side to side, swinging down with the flag.

Phoebe.

Phoebe Yamura.

Hanging upside down from the ceiling. Hanging by her feet.

Limp arms dangling.

Long black hair falling from her head.

Her body swinging from side to side, side to side.

Side to side . . .

PART FOUR

Chapter Eleven

After the Funeral

Josh struggled with the knot on his tie. "I have to get out of here," he muttered. He finally succeeded in tugging the knot down. Then he pulled off the dark blue tie and balled it up in his hands.

"Me, *too*," Mickey agreed, pulling off his dark blazer and tossing it over his shoulder.

They jumped down the steps to Lane's Funeral Home, taking them two at a time.

A pale half-moon rose over the whispering trees. The evening sky was darkening to purple. A few early stars glimmered between wisps of black cloud.

Josh sighed. "I can't take another funeral."

Mickey shook his head, following Josh across the street to Josh's car. "It's so sad. I just sat there and watched Phoebe's parents, sobbing their hearts out. What can you say? How can anyone explain it?"

Josh searched his trouser pockets for his car keys. "I'll never forget it . . ." he said softly, his voice breaking. "Phoebe up there, swinging upside down with the flag behind her. Everyone screaming and crying."

"Unreal," Mickey murmured. "Unreal. I really didn't think it was real," he said, opening the passenger door. "I thought it was a mannequin or something. You know. Some kind of dumb senior-class joke."

Josh sighed. "Not too many jokes this year," he muttered. "Only funerals."

"Do you believe it? They almost canceled graduation," Mickey said, shaking his head again, his dark hair falling over his eyes. "We'd get our diplomas, but we wouldn't have any graduation ceremony."

"I'm glad they changed their minds," Josh replied. He swallowed. "I guess."

"Oh, man," Mickey sighed. "This year was such bad news. Look. There goes the hearse."

Josh watched the long black car carrying Phoebe's body pull slowly away from the funeral home.

He dropped into the driver's seat of his own car and pulled the door shut. "I feel like driving and driving and driving, and never coming back," he told Mickey.

"Me, too," Mickey agreed, brushing his hair back with one hand, then tugging his necktie loose and unbuttoning the collar button of his white shirt. "Kick it. Let's go."

Josh turned the ignition and started the car.

He turned in surprise as the back door swung open. Matty poked his head in. "Hey—what's up?"

"What do you *mean* what's up?" Josh snapped. "What could be up? We all just sat through another funeral—right?"

Matty nodded. "Where you guys going?"

"Just for a ride. A long ride," Mickey told him. "You know. Just to clear our brains."

"Since when do you have brains?" Matty joked.

Josh frowned at him. "You're about as funny as the funeral."

"Can I come with you?" Matty pleaded. He didn't wait for an answer. He lumbered into the backseat.

"Whoa. Wait," Josh protested. "You can come only if you promise not to talk."

"Huh?"

"You heard me," Josh insisted.

"Okay. Okay." Matty did a zipping gesture across his mouth. He slammed his door shut. "Wait—!" he shouted.

"Now what?" Josh groaned.

"I closed the door on my jacket." He opened the door, tugged the jacket in, slammed the door.

"Let's go! Let's fly!" Mickey urged Josh, slapping the dashboard.

Josh shifted into Drive, started to pull away from the curb. And stopped when someone tapped on his window.

"Josie?" He rolled the window halfway down.

Josie's cheeks were puffy and stained from tears. Even in the dim evening light, Josh could see that her eyes were red-rimmed from crying.

"Wh-where are you going?" she asked in a trembling voice, leaning into the window.

"Just for a ride," Josh replied softly. "You okay? You need a lift home?"

Josie shook her head. "That's okay. I'm with Jennifer and Trisha." She motioned toward them with her head. "You coming home late?"

Josh frowned. "I don't know. We just feel like driving. You know."

Josie nodded and backed away.

Josh rolled the window up. Then he pulled away with a squeal of the tires.

"She looks pretty messed up," Mickey commented.

Josh lowered his foot on the gas. He felt like pushing it all the way down, roaring through town, pushing it until the car took off, soared over the trees.

"Josie? Yeah. I'm kind of worried about her," Josh admitted. "All these deaths—they've made her a little weird."

"They've made us *all* weird," Matty murmured from the backseat.

Mickey turned back to him. "You were *born* weird, Winger. When you were born, your mother slapped the doctor!" Mickey let out a high laugh.

"Hey—I thought we weren't allowed to make jokes," Matty protested.

"I wasn't joking!" Mickey replied, and laughed again.

"Give me a break," Josh muttered. He swerved onto the Mill Road, passed a slow-moving van, and roared up the narrow lane. "Anyway, my parents are getting Josie some help."

"I talked to one of the grief counselors the school brought in," Mickey confessed.

Josh turned to him. "You did?"

Mickey grinned. "Yeah. She was pretty *hot*. But she said she was too old for me." He slapped the dashboard with both hands.

"You're a jerk," Josh muttered, shaking his head. "Did you really come on to a grief counselor? That's sick."

Mickey grinned in reply. "Whatever."

They drove on in silence for a few minutes. Then Josh suddenly pulled to the curb.

"Where are we? The woods?" Matty asked.

"The Fear Street Woods," Josh announced. He glanced at Matty in the rearview mirror. "You're not scared—are you?"

"Yeah. For sure. I'm shaking all over," Matty replied sarcastically.

"Why'd you stop here?" Mickey demanded.

"I don't know." Josh pushed open the car door. "I thought maybe we'd take a walk down to the lake."

"Hey—we could drown Matty down there!" Mickey suggested, pretending to be excited by the idea.

Josh nodded. "Yeah. That's what I was thinking. Think anyone would come to his funeral?"

"Not funny, guys," Matty protested.

"His parents would probably be too busy," Mickey joked. "They'd probably go to a movie or something."

"Or maybe they'd have a party!" Josh exclaimed.

Matty climbed out of the car. "Do you guys know how funny you're *not*?"

Josh closed the car door and led the way to the edge of the woods. The half-moon still floated low in the sky. Black clouds covered the stars. The woods were still. The fresh spring leaves on the old trees didn't move.

"Hey, Matty—what did you do to your arm?" Mickey asked.

Josh turned to see the big bandage wrapped around Matty's elbow.

Matty shrugged. "Beats me. I guess I cut it or something. I really don't remember."

Josh studied it. "Weird."

They made their way through the tilting old trees, cutting a path through the darkness. The woods were silent except for the scrape of their shoes over the carpet of dead leaves.

Tall reeds rose up on the sloping ground as they neared Fear Lake. They could hear the gentle rush of the shallow water as it lapped against the muddy shore.

"Well. Here we are," Mickey said. "Now what?"

Josh gazed at the reflection of the half-moon in the rippling water. "I don't know. I don't know what we're doing here. At least— it's away from everything."

He took off his shoes and socks and rolled up his pants legs. Then he went wading in the cold water. The muddy bottom felt soothing on his feet. But the water still held its winter chill.

Matty and Mickey tossed stones into the lake, trying to make them skip. Josh stepped out from the lake, his pants cuffs soaked. He tromped around, waiting for his feet to dry. Then he pulled on his shoes without the socks.

"*Now* what do you want to do?" Mickey asked. "It's kind of boring down here."

"I don't mind," Josh replied solemnly. "I think I *like* boring for a change. The sight of that poor girl in the auditorium, hanging by her feet . . . I mean, we *knew* her. We saw her every day. And now . . ." His voice trailed off.

"Let's get going," Matty urged suddenly. "I don't like being out here like this. It's too weird."

Mickey turned and began trudging along the grassy bank toward the trees. "Matty is right. For once," he said. "Let's go, Josh. It's going to rain, anyway."

"Yeah. Whatever," Josh muttered. He tossed a rock into the water and watched the ripples fan out over the dark surface.

He had thought that maybe coming down here where it was so quiet, so peaceful, would help make him feel better. Help soften the tight knot in his stomach, make the lump in his throat melt away.

But it hadn't helped.

You can't run away from the real world, Josh told himself. No matter where you try to hide, your thoughts will still find you.

Josh heard a flapping sound. A soft flutter.

Then Mickey's excited shout from the woods up ahead shook him from his grim thoughts.

"Hey—guys!" Mickey called. "Hey—I've got him! I caught Clark! I caught Count Clarkula!"

Chapter Twelve

A Surprise for the Vampire

J osh and Matty hurried to catch up. Josh saw Mickey standing under a low tree branch, his hands cupped in front of him.

"Check it out!" Mickey declared. He opened his hands to reveal a small black bat.

The bat's eyes glowed wetly up at them. Its paper-thin wings lay outstretched, flat against Mickey's palm.

"It's stunned," Mickey said. "It isn't trying to fly away or anything."

"It sure is ugly," Matty declared. "It's uglier than Josh! Check out those teeth."

Two slender, pointed teeth curled out from its closed mouth. The teeth were sticky with drool.

"Let it go," Josh urged softly. "It's scared to death, Mickey."

"No way!" Mickey closed his hands over it. "Let Count Clarkula go?" The bat fluttered inside Mickey's hands. "Easy, fella."

"How'd you catch him?" Matty asked.

"Just plucked him off the tree trunk," Mickey replied. "Guess Clark was snoozing."

"Let him go," Josh repeated impatiently. "I don't want a bat in my car."

Matty scratched at the bandage on his arm. "We should do something cool with it."

"Yeah. Right." Mickey's eyes flashed. "I know. Let's take it to Clark. It's probably his cousin or something."

"Yeah. Take it to Clark. That's bold! That's bold!" Matty declared.

Josh frowned. "What's the point—"

An evil smile spread over Mickey's face. "We'll set it loose in Clark's room. Give him a surprise. He'll totally freak."

"That's totally bold!" Matty exclaimed.

"You guys have got to get a life," Josh muttered. But he didn't argue about it. Actually, he thought it was a pretty funny idea. Maybe doing something dumb like letting a bat loose in someone's house would help lift him from his unhappy thoughts.

They drove to Clark's house, laughing, joking about how Clark would totally lose it. Josh kept glancing over at the bat from behind the wheel. "I don't want any bat guano on my leather seats," he warned Mickey.

"Clark would never do that!" Mickey joked. He held the bat tightly between his hands.

It flapped its wings weakly a few times, its

little gray chest fluttering, shiny black eyes gazing up at Mickey.

Josh slowed the car to a stop at the curb in front of Clark's house. They gazed up the sloping lawn at the broad, gray-shingled house. Completely dark except for the orange glow of a small porch light.

"Maybe no one is home," Matty muttered.

"Count Clarkula is probably out flying around somewhere," Mickey said. Gripping the bat in one hand, he pushed open the car door.

Josh reached out a hand to stop him. "Where are you going? He isn't home."

"That's even better," Mickey replied, grinning again. "We'll sneak into the house and close the bat up in Clark's room. When he gets home . . ."

Josh's memory flashed back to last spring. A few weeks after school let out, the three of them had sneaked into Clark's house.

They had been searching for evidence that Clark really was a vampire. And to their shock and horror, they had found a black cape in Clark's room, along with a pile of old books about vampires, and a clump of dirt in Clark's bed.

Proof.

Except that these all turned out to be props for a surprise vampire visit at Trisha Conrad's spring party. Trisha had helped Clark buy everything he needed to portray a vampire at the party.

Not proof.

The rumors about Clark were ridiculous, Josh believed. Because Clark had black hair and pale skin, and wrote poetry and acted mysterious, kids called him Count Clarkula.

But he's no more a vampire than Matty is, Josh thought.

They sneaked into Clark's house anyway. The front door was locked. But Mickey remembered the side window they had used last spring.

They crept through the dark back hallway, floorboards creaking under their shoes. Mickey led the way, holding the bat carefully in front of him.

Matty tripped over a low table in the hall and stumbled into the wall.

"Graceful as always," Josh muttered.

The phone rang. They froze at the side of the stairs.

One ring. Two. Three.

An answering machine clicked on. "You have reached the Dickson family. . . ."

"We cannot come to the phone. We are all out drinking blood," Matty added his own words.

Josh and Mickey laughed.

The answering machine beeped. They heard a loud, steady hum. The caller had hung up.

Josh realized that his heart was pounding. His throat felt tight and dry. Why are we doing this? This is really stupid.

They made their way quickly up the stairs and then across the short hall to Clark's room. "Don't turn on a light," Mickey warned in a whisper.

"Just drop the bat in his room and close the door," Josh instructed. "We've got to get out of here."

But Mickey ignored him and carried the bat into the dark bedroom. "The window is open," he called. "Quick—close it. The bat will fly right out."

Josh followed Matty into the room. Matty slid the window shut. He turned back to them—and bumped something over.

"Hey—what was that?" Matty clicked on the desk lamp.

Just a pile of magazines, Josh saw. Horror and science-fiction magazines.

"Set the bat down and let's go," Josh urged. "We don't want to be here when—"

A cough made him stop.

Matty gasped. Mickey nearly dropped the bat.

"Hi, guys," a voice called.

Josh spun around to see Clark in the doorway. He wore black, as usual. A tight black T-shirt pulled down over black denims. His dark hair fell over one eye.

"Hey—" Josh uttered.

Clark took a step into the room. "How'd you guys get in here?"

"We . . . we brought you a present," Mickey said, unable to hold back his grin. He held out his cupped hands toward Clark.

Clark's eyes grew wide. "A present?"

"Yeah." Mickey nodded. He lifted the hand on top, revealing the bat.

"It's your cousin!" Matty declared, laughing.

The bat fluttered its thin, veiny wings against Mickey's palm.

Josh waited for Clark's startled reaction.

But Clark's expression didn't change. "Thanks, guys," he said calmly.

Josh watched Clark reach with both hands and lift the bat from Mickey's hand. Clark spread the wings out wide.

Then he raised the bat close to his face. And sank his teeth deep into the animal's gray belly.

Chapter Thirteen

Matty Helps the Vampire

Josh uttered a gasp of horror.

Gripping the wings tightly, Clark pressed the creature to his face. He made loud slurping noises as he hungrily sucked out the bat's insides.

The bat let out a high-pitched shriek. Josh saw its eyes go wide with terror. Then the eyes closed. The tiny gray head tilted lifelessly to one side.

"Mmmmm mmmmmm."

Clark groaned with pleasure as he sucked on the dead bat. Grinding his teeth over it. Swallowing noisily.

When he finally lowered the bat, he had bright red blood smeared over his chin, his cheeks.

"Clark—no!" Josh choked out. A chill ran down his back. His legs suddenly felt weak.

"You—you—" Mickey sputtered.

Matty pressed a hand over his mouth, his stomach churning noisily.

Clark smiled through the bat blood on his face. "Don't be upset, guys," he said softly. "I'm clouding your minds right now. You won't remember any of this in a few seconds."

Josh felt the vampire's eyes on him. Trapped in the powerful gaze, Josh couldn't move.

Couldn't remember . . .

Couldn't think.

How long did the trance last?

What trance?

Josh opened his eyes. He felt groggy, as if he had just been awakened from a long nap. "Hey." He shook his head hard, trying to force himself awake.

"Where's the bat?" Mickey asked Clark.

"Huh?" Matty scratched his head, his expression dazed. "Bat?"

"Yeah. Where is it?" Mickey demanded.

"It flew out the window," Clark announced. He pointed to the open window.

Wasn't that window closed? Josh asked himself.

He stared at Clark, trying to focus. Clark's face glistened wetly, as if he'd just washed it.

"Thanks for the present, guys," Clark said, shaking his head. "But next time close the window first."

All three of them stared blankly at the open window.

Josh rubbed his eyes. Why did he feel so strange?

Matty broke the silence. "Where were you?" he asked Clark. "Did you go out with Trisha tonight?"

Huh? Josh thought. Clark and Trisha? That's a joke—right?

Clark's smile faded. "We were supposed to go out. But she was too messed up. You know. About Phoebe."

Josh pictured the horrifying scene again. Phoebe hanging by her feet. Her body being lowered upside down from the ceiling of the auditorium. And her limp arms dangling . . . dangling . . .

"I'm upset, *too*," Clark murmured, lowering his eyes. "I liked Phoebe. She was really nice." He raised his eyes to them. "If only we could graduate without any more tragedies."

They all nodded.

Mickey was eyeing Clark. "You and Trisha? Are you kidding us?"

Clark frowned. For just a second his dark eyes flashed angrily. "I don't get the joke," he replied sharply.

He bent down to pick up the magazines that had fallen over. "Trisha and I may go out next Saturday. She said she'd see how she was feeling about things."

"Wow. You have a lot of weird magazines," Matty commented. "Do you really read that stuff?"

Clark nodded. "Yeah. I'm into it."

"I'm into *Star Trek*," Matty told him. "You know. The original shows. I was thinking of starting a Klingon website. But I don't have the right software."

"Hey, Matty, what planet are you from?" Mickey asked.

Matty ignored him.

"We've got to get going," Josh said.

"Yeah. See you," Mickey told Clark.

They started to the door.

"Hey, Matty—could you stay a while longer?" Clark asked. "I'll give you a lift home later. I—I need help with something."

Matty shrugged. "Yeah. Sure. No problem." He turned to Josh and Mickey. "Catch you later, guys. It's been real."

Josh and Mickey exchanged puzzled glances. Why does Clark need Matty? Matty is *useless*! Then they made their way quickly down the stairs.

They were out the front door when Josh heard a sharp cry from upstairs, a cry of pain.

He turned to Mickey. "That wasn't Matty—*was* it?"

PART FIVE

Chapter Fourteen

"Did You Hear about Trisha?"

J osie stared up at the spiny cracks across her bedroom ceiling. They branched out across the white plaster like a network of narrow, crisscrossing roads.

Wish I was in a car, driving off somewhere, Josie thought sadly. Driving off *anywhere*.

Yawning loudly, she glanced at her clock radio. Nearly one in the morning.

I'm so tired, she thought. But I can't fall asleep. I'm *afraid* to fall asleep.

It was a warm night, the air heavy and still. But Josie pulled the quilt up to her chin. I'm leaving the bed table lamp on, she decided. Like a two-year-old. I'm sleeping with the light on.

As if that will help keep away the nightmares.

As if that will help keep the evil spirit from visiting me in my dreams.

If only I could sleep one night without dreaming.

She groaned and rolled onto her side, thinking about her physics final.

My last final tomorrow, and I'll be a total wreck. Up all night. I won't be able to think straight.

She shut her eyes tighter, tried to clear her mind.

I don't want to fall asleep—but I *have* to sleep.

When will my life be normal again? After graduation?

Will it *ever* be normal?

Without realizing it, she drifted into a heavy sleep.

And saw two bare feet. The feet were tied together at the ankles. They stood straight up with a bright blue sky behind them, as if their owner was standing on her head.

The feet slid out of view. A girl appeared, standing up against the solid blue. Her straight black hair fell over her face, hiding her.

"Phoebe—is that you?" Josie asked in the dream.

The black hair rose up, blown by a strong wind. The girl's eyes were closed. Her mouth was twisted in a strange crooked sneer.

"Phoebe—?" Josie cried.

Yes. Phoebe opened her eyes and seemed to gaze straight ahead at Josie.

"Phoebe? What are you doing here?" Josie

demanded, feeling strong fright, feeling total panic. "You're . . . *dead*!"

Phoebe nodded slowly, her eyes staring blankly, her mouth still twisted in a tight, unhappy sneer.

And then Deirdre Palmer appeared beside her. Her blond hair blew wild around her face, as if buffeted by a strong blast of wind. Her green eyes glowed dully, dead eyes, sad eyes.

"Deirdre—no!" Josie gasped. "No—please. You're dead. You're both dead!"

Phoebe and Deirdre nodded slowly.

Like zombies, Josie thought, gripped with horror. Feeling so cold, frozen, even in her dream.

"What do you want?" Josie demanded.

The blue sky darkened to gray, then to a deep, swirling purple.

"*Help us, Josie*," Deirdre moaned.

"*Help us*," Phoebe repeated in a whisper.

"*Help us!*" both girls pleaded in unison.

They reached out, reached out their hands to her.

Josie awoke. Someone grabbed her shoulder.

She blinked up at her mother, leaning over her, sitting on the edge of the bed. "Huh? Mom?"

"Josie—you were crying out in your sleep. So loud, Dad and I heard you down the hall."

Josie swallowed. Pulled the quilt up around her. "I was having another nightmare."

"I know," Mrs. Maxwell said softly, smoothing the quilt over Josie. "I know how troubled you are. By everything . . . everything that's happened this year."

"Yes," Josie agreed. "Everything."

"We've arranged for you to see a really good doctor," Mrs. Maxwell said.

"Whoa—wait!" Josie pulled away. Sat up straight, her heart pounding. "A doctor? But I'm not *crazy*, Mom! I don't need a doctor!"

Her mother frowned. "Josie, no one is saying you're *crazy*. But even you admit that you're deeply troubled."

"But—but—" Josie protested weakly.

"A lot of your friends are seeing grief counselors," Mrs. Maxwell continued. "You need someone to talk to. Someone who will listen to you. Dr. Gollub will do that. She'll help you get your thoughts out. All these troubled thoughts—"

"That's not going to help!" Josie shrieked. "You don't understand, and Dr. Gollub won't, either."

"Listen to me," her mother insisted, biting her bottom lip. "Even Josh is worried about you."

"But I have a final tomorrow!" Josie cried. "My last final. And then I have to get the party together. Did you forget? I've invited the entire class. It's only a few days away!"

"I haven't forgotten," her mother replied. "But I have to insist. I'm not giving you a choice. You need to talk to someone, and—"

"Okay, okay!" Josie interrupted sharply. She could see that her mother wasn't going to back down. "Okay. I'll go see Dr. Gollub—once. I'll go once. That's it."

"Fine," Mrs. Maxwell said, standing up. She sighed. "I only want to help you."

Josie shut her eyes and pictured Phoebe and Deirdre again.

"Help us . . . help us . . ."

After the physics final Josie cornered Josh in the hall. "What are you doing now?"

Josh shrugged. "I don't know. How was your final?"

"Wonderful. I aced it," Josie replied sarcastically. "It was so great, I'll probably become a physics major at Sarah Lawrence."

"Ha ha," Josh replied, frowning at her.

She grabbed his arm. "Come on. You're coming with me."

He pulled back. "Where? What are you talking about?"

"I have to go to the mall and order food for the party. And you're going to come help me. It's your party, *too*, Josh."

"What's the big deal? I thought we were just having pizza," he protested.

"Yeah. Right. But we'll need about thirty pizzas," Josie replied impatiently. "You can't just call Pete's Pizza up when the party starts and say send over thirty pizzas." She sighed. "And we need drinks . . . and chips . . . and dessert . . . and . . . and—"

"Okay." Josh tossed up his hands in surrender. "Let's go do it now. I promised Mickey I'd stop by his house later."

Josh drove them to the Division Street Mall. They talked about finals and about graduation rehearsal. Josie started to tell him she'd agreed to see Dr. Gollub—once. But she changed her mind and stopped herself.

It's Josh's fault I have to see a shrink, she thought bitterly. I told Josh everything. And he only pretended to believe me.

As soon as they entered the mall, Josh hurried away.

"Hey—where are you going?" Josie called after him.

"I think I saw a girl I used to know!" he shouted back. He vanished around the side of Radio Shack.

Josie balled her hands into tight fists. "He promised he'd help," she grumbled.

Shaking her head, she crossed the aisle and made her way toward the pizza restaurant. She had walked only five or six steps when she saw Jennifer Fear running toward her, hair bobbing behind her as she ran.

"Josie—did you hear about Trisha?" Jennifer called. "She *died!*"

Chapter Fifteen

The Cursed School

Josie let out a startled cry and slumped back against the tile wall. Her knees started to fold. Everything went bright white.

I'm going to faint, she realized.

Jennifer hurried up to her breathlessly. "Josie—what's wrong?"

Josie swallowed hard. She took a deep breath. "You—you—" she stammered. "You said Trisha *died*!"

Jennifer tossed back her head in a laugh. "Died? I didn't say that!"

"What—?"

Jennifer rolled her eyes. "I *said*—Trisha dyed her hair. Red. Bright red." She laughed again. "Are you okay? Did you *really* think I said that Trisha *died*?"

Josie stared back at her but didn't reply. Her heart still pounded. Her mind was whirring.

Maybe I *am* cracking up, she thought. Maybe I *am* totally losing it. Now I'm starting to hear things!

"Hey—Rosanna!" Josh called to a girl up ahead. He hurtled between two women with baby strollers. "Rosanna!"

Was it the girl he used to know?

Yes.

The tall blond girl and her friend turned in the entrance to the CD store. They both shielded their eyes from the bright glare of spotlights overhead.

"Rosanna—hi!" Josh stopped in front of them, breathing hard.

"Josh? Hey—!" A surprised smile spread over her face. "Where'd you come from? I haven't seen you since . . ."

"Since camp," Josh finished the sentence for her. "When was that? Three years ago? Yeah. We were freshmen."

Rosanna nodded. "You live around here?"

"Yeah," Josh replied. "What about you?"

"Waynesbridge," Rosanna said. "Do you believe we're graduating?"

Her friend, a short, pretty girl with straight black hair, dark eyes, and three earrings dangling from each ear, cleared her throat.

"Oh, Josh—this is my friend Katrina," Rosanna said. "Josh Maxwell."

Katrina's dark eyes flashed. "Hi, Josh." She had a soft purr of a voice, like a kitten.

She is *hot*, Josh thought.

They chatted for a few minutes about summer camp and graduation and college. Josh couldn't keep his eyes off Katrina. He wondered if she was attracted to him, *too*.

Rosanna glanced at her watch. "Oh, wow. I'm late. I have to meet Jeff." She started away. Then called back an explanation. "Jeff is my boyfriend. Good luck, Josh. Call me sometime. I'm in the Waynesbridge directory. Bye, Katrina."

She disappeared past a crowd of shoppers.

Josh and Katrina remained, standing awkwardly in the CD store doorway. Josh jammed his hands into his khakis pockets. "You going in here?" he asked, motioning to the store.

"Just hanging out, I guess," Katrina replied. "So . . . you only knew Rosanna at camp?"

Josh nodded. "Yeah. For three summers."

"What are you doing *this* summer?" she asked.

"I'm working as an office temp," he told her. "Thrilling, huh? But it'll get me some money for college stuff. Books, I guess. What are you doing this summer?"

Katrina sighed. "My parents are going to France, and they're dragging me along."

"Oh, too bad. Too bad!" Josh exclaimed sarcastically. "Poor kid."

She laughed. "It sounds great, right? But you don't know my parents!"

Josh laughed a little louder than he'd

planned. Go ahead, he urged himself. She seems to like you. Ask her out.

Just do it.

"Uh . . . would you like to do something?" he blurted out. "Maybe we could get together Saturday night?"

"Sure," she replied quickly.

Yessss! He wanted to cry and pump his fist in the air.

"Where do you go to school?" she asked, brushing a strand of dark hair away from her eyes. "Do you go to Palmer?"

"No. Shadyside," he replied.

She gasped. Her smile faded.

"What's wrong?" he demanded.

"I'm sorry," she said softly, lowering her eyes. "I can't go out with you."

"Excuse me?" Josh cried. "Why—?"

"That's the cursed school," Katrina said, still avoiding his gaze. "Where everyone is dying."

"No. Hold on," Josh replied. "That's not true. I mean, yeah. There were some accidents and things this year. But there's no kind of curse."

"I . . . I've got to go," she stammered. She finally returned her gaze to him. "I'm sorry. Really. But I can't go out with you. I just can't."

She took off before Josh could reply, jogging hard, her backpack bouncing on her back.

"Wow," Josh murmured, watching her until

she disappeared around a corner. "Wow. I don't believe this."

Does everyone in town think our school is cursed? he wondered.

He suddenly remembered Josie. I've got to tell her what just happened. She won't believe it, either.

He passed the Pet Palace and the Doughnut Hole, and turned the corner toward Pete's Pizza.

He stopped with a sharp cry when he saw the girl across the hallway.

He saw her straight, white-blond hair first. Then her green eyes. Eyes he knew so well. Then her whole face came into focus.

"Noooo!" A moan escaped Josh's throat.

"Debra!"

Debra Lake.

Poor, dead Debra.

She turned. She saw him. She stretched out those delicate hands, as if reaching for him, reaching from a long, long distance.

"Debra—you're here?" he choked out, moving across the aisle, stumbling toward her. "Debra? But you died! You died, Debra!"

"*Help me, Josh.*" Her voice floated on the air, a whisper, a whisper he could barely hear over the tinny mall music.

"*Help me—please.*"

He lurched forward—and grabbed her shoulders.

"Debra! You're here!" he gasped.

"Let go of me!" she screamed.

Her angry cry startled him. "But, Debra—
it's me! I don't understand. I—"

"*Let go of me!*"

And as he stared, her face changed. The
green eyes darkened to brown. The blond
hair, so fine and light, pulled back in a dark
ponytail.

Not Debra.

He gripped her shoulders and stared.

Not Debra. Another girl. A stranger.

A stranger who began to scream in fear.
"Help! Police! Police—help me!"

Chapter Sixteen

A Surprise at the Doctor's Office

Josie stopped outside the dark wood door and took a deep breath. A small brass sign beside the door read: *Dr. Ellen Gollub. Please Ring Bell.*

Josie arranged the red vest she had pulled over a gray T-shirt, then pushed back her hair with both hands. "Okay, okay. Let's get this over with," she muttered to herself.

She pushed the doorbell beneath the sign and waited to be buzzed into the office. When there was no response after half a minute or so, she pressed the bell again.

Again no response.

She tried the doorknob. Turned it. Pushed open the door and stepped into a small, brightly lit waiting room. Her eyes swept quickly over the room—two green leather armchairs and a matching couch. A low coffee table strewn with magazines. Color photos on the walls of a tranquil-looking pond in the woods.

A small square desk in front of a door that appeared to lead to a back office. The door was open only a crack. No one at the receptionist's desk.

Is the office closed? Josie wondered. No one here?

Did I catch a break?

No. She could hear a woman's voice speaking in low, steady tones from the back office.

Josie took a seat on the edge of the couch. She crossed and uncrossed her legs. She curled a strand of her hair round and round her finger.

I never should have agreed to come here, she thought. It's a total waste of time. This woman isn't going to believe me, either.

She thought of Josh. She pictured him running up to her in the mall the day before, so pale and breathless and frightened.

"You're right, Josie," he had admitted. "I should have believed you. Something very weird is going on here. I saw Debra. I really did. I believe you now."

So you finally believe me. Too late, Josh. I'm sitting here in this shrink's office about to make a total fool of myself. Or even worse. About to prove to her that I've gone insane, that I'm a crazed lunatic because of everything that's happened at school.

I'm going, she decided. I'm outta here.

She stood up—and the voice from the back

office called out to her. "Josie Maxwell? Is that you? Come in, Josie. I can see you now."

Josie hesitated. Eyed the door to the hall-way. Then, with a sigh, turned and trudged into Dr. Gollub's office.

She was surprised to find a plump, moth-erly, middle-aged woman behind the desk. Dr. Ellen Gollub had black hair streaked with gray, pulled back tightly off her tanned fore-head into a single braid. She had big brown eyes and a full, red-lipsticked mouth pulled up in a warm smile of greeting.

The doctor wore a dark gray suit, the jacket open over a pale yellow blouse. As she shook hands with Josie, Josie noticed that her glossy fingernails matched her dark red lips.

"I'm so glad you decided to come," Dr. Gollub told Josie, holding on to her hand for a few seconds after the handshake had ended. "I spoke to your parents earlier, and I've been very eager to talk to you."

"Thanks," Josie replied. "I mean—"

Dr. Gollub motioned to the black leather couch against the wall, under several framed diplomas. "Would you like to lie down and get comfortable and talk to me?"

She must have read Josie's thoughts because she quickly added, "If you'd like, you can sit in the chair and talk. Wherever you'll be most comfortable."

Josie slid into the big leather chair. Who does she remind me of? Josie asked herself.

Someone's mother from school. Yes. Dr. Gollub looked a lot like Kenny Klein's mother.

Why am I thinking about that? Josie asked herself.

And then—*Why am I here?*

"I understand you were reluctant to come here," the doctor said, once again seeming to read Josie's thoughts. She kept her eyes on Josie as she arranged pencils in a maroon pencil case.

"Well . . ." Josie hesitated. "What I have to say sounds pretty crazy. I don't think anyone will believe me. I mean, I don't really believe it myself."

Dr. Gollub scribbled something quickly on a yellow pad. "There's been a lot of tragedy at your school this year, I understand."

Josie nodded.

"I've read about it in the newspaper," the doctor said, lowering her pencil to the desk. She squinted at Josie. "Some of your friends have died?"

Josie nodded again, feeling a lump form in her throat. "Yes," she choked out. "Several."

"And you feel . . .?" Dr. Gollub began. "Sad? Shocked? Frightened?"

"I feel responsible," Josie replied flatly, surprised by her own sudden boldness.

The answer made Dr. Gollub blink. She adjusted herself in the desk chair. "Responsible? Do you think you could explain?"

Josie clasped her hands tightly in her lap. To her surprise, she felt calmer. Less tense than when she had entered the office.

Perhaps because she said the most difficult part first? Because she didn't wait to admit that she felt responsible for the curse on the senior class?

"I guess I can explain," Josie said slowly, thoughtfully. "Do you believe in evil spirits?"

Dr. Gollub blinked again. She cleared her throat, her gaze steady on Josie. "Evil spirits? Not really."

"Neither did I," Josie continued. "Until last spring."

The doctor leaned across the desk eagerly. "What happened last spring, Josie?"

Josie licked her lips. Talking evenly, calmly, she began to tell Dr. Gollub about the little library in Jennifer Fear's house. About the Doom Spell Josie cast last June.

So long ago . . .

So many deaths ago . . .

As Josie told the story from the beginning, the room blurred into soft focus. So hazy, Josie thought. As if a thick fog filled the room.

Dr. Gollub faded into the background, faded into the soft haze of Josie's thoughts and memories.

Josie hardly heard her own voice as she talked, describing the evil, cloaked figure. "Now it's coming to me in my dreams," she said. "It will not leave me alone. It says that no one will graduate."

Josie raised her eyes to a sudden blur of motion. Why was Dr. Gollub at the office door? Did she just click the lock on the door?

It was all so hazy, so foggy, as if seeing things through a billowing white curtain.

"Of course, no one believes me," Josie continued. "I don't expect you to believe me, either. But—"

She stopped as the doctor moved quickly toward her, a blur of gray and yellow. Josie blinked hard, struggling to focus her eyes.

When the fog finally lifted and she could see clearly again, she froze in horror.

Dr. Gollub's red lips pulled back into a snarl. The lips pulled back, and the mouth gaped wider . . . wider . . .

Josie saw grinning teeth. Then the bone of the jaw. The skin on the woman's face slid back, as if someone was pulling it off the skull.

"Noooooo!" A low moan escaped Josie's throat.

Dr. Gollub tugged her face off with both hands, revealing a cracked yellowed skull. Her eyeballs popped wetly from their sockets and bounced onto the carpeted office floor.

The skin flaked and peeled off her arms, her hands, revealing gray bones that clacked and clicked as the hands reached out for Josie.

Josie's mouth dropped open in horror as the twin snakes slid out from the skull's empty eye sockets.

"You—!" Josie gasped. "You're here! Nooooo! No—please! Let me go!"

Josie lurched from the chair. The room tilting, the floor spinning, she dived to the door.

No escape.

Hissing, snapping their jaws, the snakes shot out from the grinning skull. Stretching . . . longer . . . longer . . .

As Josie tried to duck past, they wrapped themselves around her waist—tightened themselves around her, tightened, tightened and pulled.

"I—I can't breathe!" Josie gasped, tugging at the snakes with both hands. Trying to free herself from their grasp.

She couldn't fight them.

They pulled her. Pulled her toward the skeletal figure.

Hissing and snapping at her hands, they pulled her in, like a fish on a line.

Until she stood face-to-face with the evil creature.

"Come inside! Come inside!" the yellowed skull rasped, the broken teeth clicking in her face. Hot, sour breath washed over her, sickening her.

"Come inside!"

Chapter Seventeen

Josie Dies

"**N**ooooo—let go!" Josie shrieked in a high, shrill cry of terror, of anger . . . of disgust.

The twin snakes tightened around her waist, choking her, cutting through her clothes, her skin . . . wrapping her in burning pain.

"*Come inside!*" the grinning skull rasped, sending another blast of hot, sour breath over Josie's face. "*Come inside!*" A hoarse whisper that sounded like metal scraping against metal.

The jaws opened wide.

Josie could see worms crawling behind the teeth, over the roof of the mouth. She heard insects buzzing, the sound rising and falling from somewhere deep inside the evil spirit.

"*Come inside . . . Come inside . . .*"

Gasping for air, pain throbbing up and down her body, she struggled to escape. She thrashed her arms. Pounded her fists against the creature's bony ribs. Squirming and twisting in the tightening snake grasp, she tried to kick, tried to squeeze free.

And then she felt herself lifted off the floor. Her feet swinging helplessly.

Can't breathe . . . Can't breathe . . .

Too much *pain* to breathe.

She had no choice. She surrendered to it. Surrendered to the darkness.

The clicking jaws swung open wide. Josie was lifted . . . carried inside . . .

So cold and dark now. As if no heat or light had ever been allowed in here.

She slid headfirst, slowly at first, then picking up speed until she felt herself hurtling down, down through the frozen murk.

Where am I? she wondered. This can't be happening.

I'm falling . . . falling through *what*?

And then all thoughts stopped. She couldn't form words. She couldn't see or think.

She became an object plunging down . . . down . . .

Into mournful howls and moans of pain. The cries rising all around her, sweeping around her—then *through* her. Until she became the sound.

Was she howling in agony? Or was someone howling through her?

The howls faded behind low moans of horror.

The cries of the dead?

Grinning skulls, cracked and eyeless, bobbed around her. They tilted and twirled, bounced off her, as the moans faded into a steady wail, rising and falling like a siren.

Down . . .

Past ugly, monstrous faces, twisted in pain. Glowing green faces, distorted, with skin dripping, mouths open, howling, howling in a never-ending symphony of horror.

So much evil.

And I'm inside it.

And then—blackness.

So solid. So heavy and silent.

No howls or moans now. No bouncing skulls or faces crying out their agony.

Silence.

Black silence.

I'm dead, Josie realized.

I died.

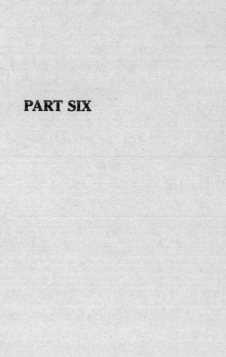

PART SIX

Chapter Eighteen

Evil Behind the Wheel

Josie blinked.

Harsh light invaded her eyes. She shut them and waited for the pain to fade.

Her whole body trembled. She could feel her muscles, all taut, all clenched tightly, begin to loosen.

When she opened her eyes again, she saw white curtains. The curtains flapped and fluttered noisily even though the window was closed.

That's impossible, she thought.

She opened her mouth, tried to speak. But her throat was so dry, so achingly dry. Like sandpaper.

Only a hoarse cough escaped her throat.

She blinked again.

Where am I? I'm sitting on a floor. My hands are cold. I'm so cold . . . and tired. I—

"How did you get in here?"

The harsh woman's voice made Josie jump.

The curtains dropped in place in front of the window and didn't move.

Josie turned, her hands still resting on the soft carpet. She raised her gaze and saw a young woman standing in a doorway. The woman had frizzed-out red hair that tumbled down over a pale blue sleeveless top. She wore loose-fitting, faded denim jeans and sandals.

"How did you get in the office?" she repeated, staring down at Josie, a clipboard pressed against her chest.

"Office?"

Josie blinked again. Cleared her throat. Began to focus.

She pulled herself onto her knees. Turned and saw the doctor's dark desk. The black leather couch against the wall. The leather armchair where she had told the doctor about the evil spirit . . .

The evil spirit?

The red-haired woman squinted down at Josie, waiting for an answer.

"I—I have an appointment," Josie stammered, finally finding her voice.

"Are you okay?" the woman asked, her eyes still narrowed. "Can I help you up?"

"No. I think I can do it." Josie pulled herself unsteadily to her feet. The room tilted to the right, then the left, then straightened itself out.

The young woman pulled the clipboard from her chest and ran a finger down a sheet of paper. "You're Josie Maxwell?"

Josie nodded. "Yes. I—"

"Well, how did you get in?" the woman asked again.

Josie returned the woman's stare. "The doctor called me in," she told her.

"Excuse me? The doctor?" The woman's expression turned suspicious. She lowered the clipboard to her side. Then she tossed her head sharply, sending the frizzed-out red hair flying back over her slender shoulder. "That's impossible."

"What do you mean?" Josie demanded.

"Dr. Gollub called in sick today. Didn't you get the message? She canceled all of her appointments."

"No. I didn't get the message," Josie murmured, her heart suddenly racing.

And then, before she even realized what she was doing, she took off running.

She pushed past the startled young woman and burst through the office doorway. Out into the empty waiting room.

"Hey, wait—! Wait a minute!"

Ignoring the woman's cries, Josie ran down the long hall of the office building. Out the exit. And kept running. Across the parking lot, empty except for her mom's car and one other parked across from it.

The afternoon sun, hot and bright, still high in the cloudless sky.

Her shoes thudding loudly on the parking lot pavement. Sunlight bouncing in front of her. Her shadow, long and pale, sliding beside her as she ran.

The evil spirit followed me here, she realized.

It waited for me here. Tricked me. Tried to swallow me.

It's after me now, she told herself. I'm the only one who can stop it—and it's going to stop me first.

I'm not going to survive graduation. Unless I can find a way to stop it.

But how? How?

Panting hard, she lurched up to the car and grabbed the door handle.

"Owwww!"

She cried out as seering heat burned through her hand.

"Too hot—"

She jerked back her hand. Tried to pull it off the burning chrome handle.

But her hand stuck there as if glued on.

"Owwwww." She tugged. Pulled with her whole body.

"It's *scalding* me!"

And then, as she squirmed and struggled, Josie peered through the curtain of sunlight on the car window.

Peered inside—and saw the red-cloaked figure in the driver's seat. The bony hands caressed the wheel. The skull turned beneath its hood and grinned out at her.

"No—please! Let me go! Let me go!" she shrieked through the sobs that burst from her throat. "Why are you torturing me?"

The heat from the door handle burned through the tender skin on her hand. The sharp, throbbing pain shot up her arm. Made her whole body shake.

The evil figure rocked gleefully back and forth behind the wheel, head tossed back, rotted jaws sliding up and down as if laughing.

Laughing in triumph.

The bony hands slapped the wheel.

"Owww. Let me go. My hand—it's burning . . . burning up . . ." Josie moaned.

She gave a final, desperate tug.

Too late.

With a deafening roar, the car exploded into flame.

Chapter Nineteen

Dead Seniors

White light blinded Josie.

The force of the blast heaved her up into the air—and dropped her several yards across the parking lot.

She landed hard on her back. Felt her breath knocked out.

A sharp stab of pain at her wrist made her sit up.

"My hand—!" She gasped.

She pictured it still gripping the car door handle.

Her hand—ripped off in the blast of flames.

But no. She stared down at it. Stared at her hand. Still attached. She wriggled the fingers, made a trembling fist.

Halfway across the lot, tall flames danced and crackled over the car.

Mom's car . . . Josie thought.

No way she'll understand.

Inside the leaping orange and yellow flames, the cloaked skeleton rocked behind the wheel, slapping the skeletal hands in a wild rhythm, laughing, laughing in a wild, high cackle that rose up over the roar of the fire.

"No . . . oh, no . . ." Sitting on the hot pavement in the shadow of the dancing flames, Josie buried her face in her hands.

"No . . . please . . ."

She opened her eyes when the roar of the fire stopped.

What did she expect to see? Ashes? Metal burned black?

Instead, the car stood shiny and blue.

Empty.

No evil spirit slapping the wheel. No damage from the fire. Not a scratch. Not a burn mark.

Josie rose on trembling legs. She made her way slowly, cautiously to the car.

No damage.

No sign of the fire.

With a relieved sigh she touched the door handle—a darting touch.

Not hot.

She touched the window glass.

Not hot.

She peered into the car, her eyes stopping at the driver's seat. At the object resting on the driver's seat.

A maroon graduation cap.

Josie tilted her graduation cap back on her head. She shifted the white tassel away from her eyes. Then she pulled open the auditorium door and stepped inside.

"Hey—" She bumped into Dana Palmer, whose tassel had become tangled in a button on her maroon robe.

Dana uttered an angry curse and tugged at the tassel.

"Here. Let me help you," Josie offered.

She gazed around the crowded auditorium before leaning down to work at Dana's robe button. Seniors in maroon robes were clustered in small groups, standing in the aisles, sprawled over the seats, laughing and talking loudly.

Josie sighed. What horror is going to stop the laughter? she wondered. What does the evil spirit plan for our graduation rehearsal today?

She brought her face close to Dana's robe and began to untangle the tassel. "How did you do this? It's all knotted."

"I have no idea," Dana replied sharply. "Why do we have to rehearse this stupid thing anyway? All we have to do is walk in single file and get our stupid diplomas. Do they really think we don't know how to walk?"

Josie shrugged. She knew that Dana wasn't really upset about a tangled cap tassel or about having to rehearse. Dana was upset because her twin sister wasn't there to graduate with her.

"There you go," Josie said, pulling the tassel free.

"Thanks, Josie," Dana said softly. And then suddenly she threw her arms around Josie and hugged her, hugged her tightly, pressing her hot cheek against Josie's.

Startled, Josie hugged her back. "I know, I know," she whispered. "Deirdre was my best friend."

Dana turned quickly and hurried down the aisle.

Poor Dana, Josie thought. She's an emotional wreck.

I think we all are. I think we'll all be so glad when graduation is over and we are *out* of this school.

If the evil spirit lets us graduate.

Josie hadn't forgotten the urgency. She needed a plan, a way to stop the red-cloaked monster before it attacked again.

She needed help.

But who could help her? Who would believe her?

She searched for Josh, but couldn't find him in the sea of maroon robes and bobbing square caps.

She saw Mickey Myers down near the stage. He had his arms around some girl. Another senior that Josie didn't know too well. Zella something.

Josie hoped that Dana wasn't watching.

Mickey had Zella trapped in his arms and was tickling her with both hands. She laughed and tried to squirm free.

Josie sighed. Mickey never changes, she

thought. If Dana sees him kidding around with Zella like that, she'll be crushed.

At the end of the third or fourth row of seats, Josie saw Matty Winger sitting quietly by himself, his head down as if he were napping.

What's his problem? Josie wondered. It's not like Matty to sit quietly at an event like this. Why isn't he goofing around, making bad jokes, acting like his geeky self?

A few rows behind Matty, Josie saw Trisha and Clark, leaning close together, both talking at once.

Trisha and Clark?

Josie watched them for a while. They're not really a couple—are they? Trisha hasn't totally lost it—has she?

I need to talk to Trisha, Josie decided. I'm one of the few people who knows Trisha's secret. I know that Trisha is actually a Fear. Maybe . . . just maybe she knows something or can do something to help defeat the evil spirit.

Where is Josh? Is that him across the auditorium talking with Kenny Klein?

The loudspeaker let out a deafening, ear-shattering squeal.

Kids cried out in protest.

Mr. Montgomery, the senior adviser, appeared behind the stand-up microphone onstage. "Just trying to get your attention!" he declared.

Several seniors laughed. The rest ignored him and continued their conversations.

Mr. Montgomery tapped the microphone. He was a short, squat guy, built like a bull with a face to match. Behind his back, the kids all called him Mongo.

"The sooner we start, the sooner we'll be finished," he announced.

The loudspeaker squealed again.

"The sooner we finish, the sooner we can start partying!" Mickey Myers declared.

Several kids let out raucous cheers.

Mickey still had his arms around Zella's waist.

Josie spotted Josh a few rows behind Trisha and Clark. She waved to him, but he didn't appear to see her.

"Come on, everyone," Mr. Montgomery pleaded, scratching his close-shaved hair. "We just have to go over the order of the program, then practice marching in to the music. I'll have you out of here in twenty minutes, tops, if we can all get started now."

"Mr. Mongo?" someone called.

Laughter swept over the auditorium, echoing off the high walls.

"I mean, Mr. Montgomery?"

Josie turned to the voice. It was Kenny Klein.

Mr. Montgomery shielded his eyes with one chubby hand and gazed down at Kenny. "Yes? What is it?"

"I don't have to rehearse my valedictorian speech today—do I?"

Josie heard a few groans.

"No. Practice it at home," the teacher replied. "We don't want you to spoil the surprise for us!"

Big laughter and cheers.

Kenny laughed, *too*. He seemed very relieved.

"Okay, people!" Mr. Montgomery shouted, popping his p's in the microphone. "Here's how we're going to proceed. We're all going to line up and—"

He stopped as an explosion of loud music suddenly burst from the loudspeakers.

Josie recognized the music at once—*Pomp and Circumstance*—the music they play at all graduations.

"Whoa! Stop! We're not ready for that!" Mr. Montgomery screamed.

The music was so loud, Josie could barely hear him. She covered her ears. Several other kids covered their ears, *too*.

"Turn it off!" Mr. Montgomery screamed. "Somebody! Too soon! Too soon!"

Josie glimpsed something move at the back of the auditorium. Still holding her ears against the roar of the music, she turned and saw the auditorium doors fly open.

A maroon-gowned figure stepped into the auditorium, walking slowly, steadily, in time to the music.

Someone in the class is really late, Josie thought.

But then she saw another figure in cap and gown march in behind the first figure.

And then a third and a fourth.

Walking slowly, swaying slightly with each step, moving down the aisle to the music.

"Who is back there?" Mr. Montgomery demanded, shouting over the deafening blare from the loudspeakers. "Somebody—turn off that music!"

The marching figures had their square, maroon caps tilted over their heads. As they made their way closer, the caps tilted back.

Josie uttered a scream of horror as their grinning, ghoulish, rotting faces came into view.

Shrieks and screams rose over the music, echoed off the walls of the auditorium.

All down the row, skeletal faces stared straight ahead as the gowned figures marched. Chunks of skin had rotted away, revealing gray bone underneath. Eyes had sunken deep into sockets. Green and blue mold sprouted from noses and ears.

The sour stench of death floated over the auditorium.

Josie pressed her hands to her cheeks and screamed again.

"They're *dead*!" she heard Trisha shriek. "Oh, no! Oh, no! They're all *dead*!"

"They're *back*!" someone else cried.

"No—please!" Kenny Klein was waving his arms frantically, as if trying to wave them away, make them disappear. "Please—please—!"

But the decaying figures continued their

march, moving slowly, stiffly, hands hidden in the folds of their gowns, maroon graduation caps sliding and bouncing on their rotting skulls.

Corpses . . . Marching corpses . . .

Frozen in terror, hands pressed against her cheeks, Josie stared at the first in line—and recognized her.

Debra!

Staring blankly, lifelessly straight ahead through her sunken eyes, Debra shuffled past Josie.

And then Josie recognized the next figure. And the next.

Danielle . . . Marla . . . Ty . . . Deirdre . . . Gary . . . Phoebe . . .

The dead seniors. Her dead classmates.

Ohhh . . . the stench. The mold growing on their faces. The sunken eyes . . .

Josie started to gag.

Her stomach heaved.

She couldn't fight it down. She bent over and threw up into the aisle. Her stomach heaved and heaved.

The dead kids marched past her without slowing. Without seeing.

The dead seniors . . . marching down the auditorium aisle, all back for graduation.

Chapter Twenty

"What Can We Do?"

Still bent over, trying to catch her breath, trying to swallow away the sour taste in her mouth, Josie listened to the horrified shrieks and wails of her classmates.

"Debra—no! Debra? Is it really you?"

"Look—it's Gary. But his face—it—it's *rotted away*!"

"They're dead! They're all dead!"

"Where are they going? Can't somebody *stop* them?"

Then, over the cries of shock and disbelief, she heard a new sound.

Thunder, she thought.

She pulled herself to her feet—and realized she heard the thunder of shoes over the concrete floor. The thunder of kids stampeding for the doors.

Her eyes blurred as she stared at the

swirling maroon gowns, the graduation caps falling off, the terrified, screaming faces.

A billowing red ocean, she thought.

As red as blood . . .

And still the dead seniors marched and the loudspeakers roared.

Screams and cries of horror all around. And the thunder of shoes running up the aisles.

Josie joined the stampede, pulling up her long gown with both hands as she followed the other seniors to the doors.

Screams and sobs. Cries of horror and disbelief.

Nearly to the door Josie glanced back. And saw a gowned figure at the microphone onstage.

Marla? Marla Newman?

Yes. Josie recognized Marla's red hair.

Her bony, toothless jaws were moving up and down as she leaned her decayed face to the microphone.

What is she doing? Josie wondered. Is she giving her valedictorian speech?

And then Josie was pushed out into the hall. Pushed down the dimly lit corridor. Swimming . . . swimming in a maroon tidal wave of terror . . .

Gasping for breath, struggling to swallow despite her dry, clogged throat, Josie found herself outside.

A cool, dark night. Trees swaying in a whispering breeze. A few dim stars in a purple-black sky.

She grabbed Trisha by the shoulder. "Help me." The words burst from her aching throat before she even thought them.

Startled, pale, her chin trembling, Trisha spun around to face her. "Josie—?"

"You've got to help me now," Josie pleaded.

"Josie? We're out. We're okay!" Trisha's eyes burned into hers. "Are you okay?"

"No," Josie replied, still clinging to the shoulder of Trisha's maroon gown. "No, I'm not. I'm not okay. We're not okay, Trisha. None of us. We're not okay."

Over Trisha's shoulder Josie glimpsed screaming kids, running across the lawn, running to the parking lot, to the street.

"Josie—" Trisha started. "We've got to get away from here. Those kids . . . those dead kids . . ."

"We've got to do something now!" Josie insisted. "We don't have much time, Trisha. You've got to help me. You're a Fear. You're the only one who can help me destroy the evil!"

Trisha's mouth dropped open. "But— what can we do, Josie?" she asked in a tiny voice.

Josie shut her eyes. "I don't know. I thought we could cast another spell. But the books—Jennifer's books—they're all gone."

Cars squealed away. Shouts and cries still echoed over the school grounds and down Park Street.

Trisha shook her head. "What can we do? What can we do?" she murmured, as if chanting.

Josie suddenly had an idea. "The Fear mansion," she said.

Trisha narrowed her eyes at her. "Huh? What about it?"

"Maybe there's a clue there," Josie suggested.

"That burned-out old house? What could we possibly find there?"

Josie shrugged. "I don't know, Trisha. I'm desperate. I'll try anything. That old mansion—it's seen so much evil. So much evil started in that house. Maybe there's something there—*anything*—that might help us."

Trisha's eyes were on the school. Were the ghoulish corpses—the corpses of their friends—going to come back outside?

"So you want to go digging around in that creepy old mansion?" she asked Josie, her chin trembling again.

Josie nodded. "Come on, Trisha. Help me. Please. Come with me. I can't think of anything else to do."

"It's crazy," Trisha replied, shaking her head. "It's totally crazy." And then she added, "Let's go."

Chapter Twenty-one

The Door to Doom?

A ncient trees leaning over the road formed a dark awning over Fear Street. Little moonlight could filter through the thick leaves and branches. The trees always made Fear Street seem darker than any other place in Shadyside.

The streetlight in front of the Fear mansion had been smashed by a rock. Shards of glass littered the curb. The old house stood over the sloping, weed-choked lawn, black against an even blacker sky.

Trisha jerked her car to a stop. Cut the lights and engine.

The two girls stepped out into a strong wind that brushed against them hard, pushing them back as if trying to keep them away from the house.

Their graduation robes ruffled in the wind. Josie had forgotten she was still wearing it.

141

She and Trisha pulled their robes over their heads, revealing jeans and T-shirts underneath. They tossed the robes into the backseat of Trisha's car.

And stared up at the dark mansion, resting on its hill like a huge, silent creature. The fire—a hundred years ago—had destroyed the left half of the mansion and most of the roof. One wall had completely caved in. Tall weeds and grass had grown over it, invading the house.

No one had ever tried to repair or restore Simon Fear's old mansion. Few in town dared go near it.

Kids were always challenging each other to go inside, to stay inside for ten minutes, to spend a night there. But not many accepted the dare. Strange howls and animal cries could still be heard from the house, according to Fear Street neighbors.

And many people believed that even after it had been deserted for a hundred years, the house still held powerful evil.

"I have a flashlight in the trunk," Trisha said, her voice a whisper. The wind raised her blond hair over her shoulders. She bent over the open trunk and pulled out a small flashlight. "We'll have to share."

Josie shuddered. "That's okay. We should stick close together."

They started up the sloping lawn, their shoes sinking in the dirt, slipping on the dew-wet weeds.

"What should we look for?" Trisha asked, the light from the flashlight darting over the ground ahead of them.

"I don't know," Josie sighed, feeling a heavy knot form in her stomach as they stepped up to the house. "Maybe a book of spells. Maybe a symbol of some kind. There's got to be some way to defeat the evil spirit. If we can just find a clue here, maybe—"

The light suddenly dived, like a bird hitting the grass. Josie saw the flashlight bounce out of Trisha's hand.

Trisha dropped to her knees.

Josie stumbled over a rock. Struggled to keep her balance, her arms flailing out. "Huh? Trisha—?" she gasped.

Even in the solid darkness, she could see the dazed expression on Trisha's face, her mouth open wide, her eyes blank, rolled up in her head.

"Trisha—? Trisha—?" Josie reached for Trisha's hand. Started to tug her to her feet. Then stopped.

Josie's heart pounded as she waited for her friend to come out of her psychic vision.

Somewhere down the block, a cat cried. Or was it a child?

Josie gazed up at the dark mansion rising above her. Did something move in an upstairs window? She heard a clattering sound from inside the house.

Just an old window blind blown by the

wind, she told herself. Or maybe squirrels or rabbits have invaded the burned-out house.

Trisha stirred. A low moan escaped her throat. "The door!" she cried. "The door!"

"Huh?" Josie gasped. "What did you say? Trisha—what do you see?"

"The door!" Trisha repeated, still in her trance, her eyes still rolled up. "Yes! The door!"

Josie leaned down next to her friend, lowered her face to Trisha's. "What door? Can you tell me? What door?"

Trisha didn't reply. And then her mouth began to move stiffly up and down, like a puppet's. And a strange low voice—not Trisha's voice—burst from her throat.

"*Help me. Help me out of here.*"

Josie gasped. "Trisha—stop talking like that. You're scaring me!"

"*Help me!*" the gravelly, low voice repeated.

Josie stared at her friend. It's not Trisha talking, she realized. She didn't know what to do.

"Trisha!" Josie screamed.

No answer.

Trisha blinked several times, and her eyes rolled back into view. She closed her mouth. Licked her lips. Shook her head hard as if trying to clear it.

Then she turned to Josie. "Wow," she murmured.

"What did you see?" Josie demanded

eagerly. "Did you see something that could help us?"

"I—I don't know," Trisha replied shakily. "I saw . . . a door."

"A door?"

Trisha nodded. She allowed Josie to help tug her to her feet. "A wooden door with a crack running right down the center of it."

"And what was behind the door?" Josie asked, holding on to her friend.

"I—I don't know," Trisha stammered. "I didn't open it. I didn't see what was behind it."

"I heard a voice," Josie told her. "It came from you, but it wasn't your voice. It asked for help. It said, 'Help me out of here.'"

Trisha narrowed her eyes, struggling to remember. "Yes. I heard it, *too*," she declared finally. "A man's voice. Yes. I heard it."

"Was he . . . behind the door?" Josie demanded. "Did you see his face, Trisha?"

"No. I only heard him."

Josie bent to pick up the flashlight. "Let's go inside," she urged, ignoring a chill that ran down her back. "Let's see if we can find the cracked door."

Trisha nodded and took the flashlight from her. She raised the circle of light to the double front doors. Then she slid it along the charred front wall to the side of the mansion.

"This way," Trisha murmured, and took off, jogging across the grass.

"Hey—wait up!" Josie called. "Where are

you going?"

"This way. Follow me," Trisha replied without turning back. She jumped over a fallen tree limb, pushed away a clump of tall reeds, and kept jogging.

Josie followed her friend around the side of the house. "Trisha—I thought we were going inside!" she protested. "Why are you going this way?"

A thick tangle of thorn bushes had grown over the side of the house. Trisha tore through them, crying out as thorns scratched at her bare arms.

"Trisha—wait!" Josie called. She ducked her head and forced her way through the tall, scratchy plants.

"I have such a strong feeling," Trisha murmured, sweeping her flashlight beam along the rutted, rotting shingles and shattered windows. "Such a strong feeling."

She stopped suddenly.

Running to keep up, Josie crashed into her. "Ow! Sorry."

She turned to see why Trisha had stopped. And stared at the heavy wooden door, hidden in deep shadow near the back of the mansion.

Trisha ran the light along the deep rut, a dark crack that appeared to split the door in two.

"This is it, Josie," she whispered. "This is the door I saw."

"Whoa." Josie struggled to catch her

breath. Her whole body trembled. She shoved her hands into her jeans pockets. "You're sure?"

Trisha nodded solemnly. She reached out and ran her fingers down the jagged crack in the wood. "Yes. I saw this door. I saw it so clearly."

Josie hesitated, staring at the splintery crack.

"Should we . . . try to open it?"

Trisha bit her bottom lip. The light trembled in her hand.

Somewhere nearby the cat cried again. Such a human cry.

A warning?

"We have no choice," Trisha murmured. "We have to open it. We have to see what's on the other side."

Josie shut her eyes and took a deep breath.

Then she grabbed the rusted doorknob with both hands.

And, pulling with all her strength, tugged the door open.

Chapter Twenty-two

"I Summon Thee"

Josie heard a loud *whoosh*.

She tried to pull back. Too late.

She felt herself sucked inside.

Trisha grabbed for her. Missed.

They both lurched into the darkness, drawn in by a powerful force.

"Oh—!" Josie cried out as the door slammed behind them.

"No—! Where are we?"

Bony hands clicked and scraped, reaching for them. Hundreds of skeletal hands reaching, grasping.

Cold. It's so cold in here, Josie thought.

Low moans rose out of the darkness.

She felt a tingling on the back of her neck. Her skin crawled. She pictured hundreds of insects scuttling over her neck, her shoulders, down her back.

"Let us out!" Trisha shrieked.

They both swung back to the door. Gone. The door had vanished, replaced by inky blackness.

The bony hands clicked and scraped. Hands on long, bony arms. Faces bobbed up in the thick blackness. Ghoulish faces, eyeless, toothless, mouths open in endless moans, mournful howls.

Josie remembered being pulled inside the evil spirit. Remembered the howls and cries in that dark world.

And now I am back in that world of evil, she thought. With no door. No way to escape.

A bony hand swiped at her. Cold, wet fingers slid along her cheek.

She gasped. Fell back.

Nothing to fall back against.

She and Trisha were surrounded now by howling faces, by clicking skeletal hands.

And then a strong voice broke over the moans and howls. "*Help me.*"

The ugly, eyeless faces appeared to fade as a young man loomed in front of them. Even in the solid blackness, Josie could see that he was handsome, with wavy blond hair that fell over a broad forehead, serious dark eyes.

"*Help me,*" he repeated, his eyes moving from Josie to Trisha. Josie recognized the voice.

"Who are you?" Josie choked out, her voice hollow, dying against the darkness.

"My name? It's Henry Conrad." He turned his dark gaze on Trisha.

She uttered a startled gasp. "Conrad? But *my* name is Conrad!"

"I know," he replied softly. His dark eyes glowed. He moved closer to them. "I am your great-grandfather, Trisha."

Trisha blinked, trying to take this in. "How do you know my name?"

Henry didn't answer. He took Trisha's hand between both of his. A tender gesture. "I am your great-grandfather," he repeated softly.

"Where are we?" Trisha demanded. "How do I know you're telling the truth?"

Henry's expression turned solemn. He let Trisha's hand fall from his. "I don't know where we are," he said softly, lowering his eyes. "I only know it is a place of evil."

"We have to get out—" Josie started.

"You have to help me," Henry pleaded, turning to Josie. "I am being pursued. The Fear family—they are coming after me. They will not let me rest."

"Wh-what can we do?" Josie stammered.

"Take me out of here," Henry replied quickly. "Take me to safety. I cannot leave this place on my own. I cannot leave unless you take me out."

"We can't!" Trisha cried. "We don't know the way out."

"And we don't know if we can trust you." Josie studied his handsome face. Watched him brush a strand of blond hair off his eyes.

"You said this is a place of evil," Josie continued. "Why are you here?"

"The Fears sent me here. And now they are coming for me," Henry replied, his voice breaking. He grabbed Trisha's hand. "Please—trust me. Take me out of this place. You are my great-granddaughter. Help me. I'll return the favor. I promise I will."

Josie narrowed her eyes at him. He was tall and slender and wore a dark, old-fashioned-styled suit, high collar, and broad necktie.

"How will you return the favor?" she demanded. "Trisha and I—we have to fight a powerful evil. Can you help us?"

"Yes," Trisha said, studying her great-grandfather. "If we take you out of here, will you help us fight an evil spirit?"

"Yes," Henry replied with emotion. "Yes, yes, yes. Of course I will. I swear I will help." He raised his right hand as if swearing an oath.

Josie and Trisha exchanged glances.

Is he telling the truth? Josie wondered. He seems so frightened, so eager.

"He's my great-grandfather," Trisha whispered. "We have to help him."

Josie nodded in agreement. "Okay. You're right." She turned to Henry. "Do you know the way out?"

A smile spread across the young man's handsome face. "Yes. Follow me. Stay close. I can lead the way, but you have to take me out."

As they began to follow him through the heavy, cold gloom, the ugly, cycless faces loomed up again, and the bony hands reached out of nowhere, snapping, clicking, grabbing at them.

Up ahead, Josie saw a strange, hulklike figure, big, transparent, arms outstretched, floating quickly toward them like a jellyfish through water.

And before Josie could move or even cry out, the creature dived forward—and spread itself around her.

She staggered back under its weight. Cold. So cold. It wrapped itself around her like slimy, wet Jell-O.

Wrapped her inside . . . wrapped her . . . smothering her, spreading thickly, wet and sticky.

Can't breathe . . . Can't . . .

Josie tried to inhale—and sucked a gelatinous mass into her nose and mouth.

Choking . . . It's choking me to . . . death.

And then suddenly, as she began to fade, as she felt herself begin to lose consciousness—it was off.

Gone.

Lifted away. And she could breathe again. She opened her mouth. Spit out a mouthful of disgusting goo.

And breathed.

And then gazed up at Henry, who held the translucent, wet mass above his head, pressing it between his hands. Pressing it . . . until it popped—and a million rubbery droplets showered onto the floor.

"Thank you," Josie whispered, still tasting the bitter wetness in her mouth. "Thank you, Henry."

She realized he had saved her life.

He nodded, his dark eyes flashing.

And when Josie turned, she saw the door again. The cracked door. Rising up in front of them.

"Open it. You must open it and let me out," Henry instructed. "Or else the Fears will have me in their grasp forever."

Trisha didn't hesitate. She grabbed the rusted doorknob. Twisted it. And pushed the door open.

Josie heard another loud, startling *whoosh*. This one pushed them outside. All three of them.

She stumbled forward.

Smelled the cool, evening air. Saw the lovely shimmer of dew on the grass under the pale moonlight.

Yes!

Back outside the Fear mansion. Back in the real, familiar, sweet world.

Yes!

Josie turned and caught the happy, relieved smile on Trisha's face. And then she saw Henry, blond hair bobbing on his head, the tails of his old-fashioned suit jacket flapping as he trotted toward the front yard.

Ran without looking back.

"Hey—where are you going?" Josie called.

"Henry—come back!" Trisha cried. "You

promised us! You promised you'd help!"

He stopped at the corner of the house. And turned back to them. "I will help you as I promised," he replied stiffly.

"How—?" Trisha started.

"When you need me," Henry instructed, his hair blowing wildly around his handsome face. "When you need me, recite these words three times—*I summon thee!*"

He vanished around the side of the house. But they heard his voice call to them, "Don't worry. You haven't seen the last of me!"

And then he was gone.

PART SEVEN

Chapter Twenty-three

Clark and Trisha

'm so thirsty, Clark thought.

He turned his eyes away from Trisha. Did she notice that I've been staring at her throat?

Such a pale throat. I can see the little blue veins throbbing. Throbbing. All that rich, warm blood. Making me so thirsty.

"Well, come in," Trisha said with a laugh. "Don't just stand there in the doorway. I won't bite."

But *I* will, Clark thought, following her into the luxurious marble entryway.

He had been to the Conrads' enormous mansion overlooking the river only once before. He was totally amazed by the size of the rooms, the high ceilings, the colorful fabrics, the paintings, the beautiful, old furniture.

He felt as if he were a visitor in a museum here. Should he take off his shoes before walking on the polished wood floors and Oriental carpets?

With all this luxury, how had Trisha stayed so nice? Clark wondered. She was like a regular person, not stuck-up at all.

She was so sweet. And he knew her blood would be sweet, *too*.

Rich and sweet.

And he needed to drink so badly.

Why the sudden, overwhelming thirst? Clark asked himself.

It wasn't just Trisha's long, beautiful throat. It had to be because of all that had happened to the senior class. So much death this year. So much blood . . .

It was hard not to be thirsty.

He had made a mistake with Matty Winger. He had intended to drink only a few ounces. Maybe a pint.

But he had nearly drained Matty dry.

Did anyone notice how pale and lifeless Matty appeared?

Would they be able to trace Matty's problem to Clark?

Dangerous, Clark thought, as he followed Trisha down the long hallway to the book-lined, mahogany-shelved study.

Dangerous. It's all so dangerous. But I'm too thirsty to hold back.

Last night he had grabbed the neighbor's dog. Ripped out its throat. Drunk it dry, lapping crazily, smearing the warm blood over his face.

When the back porch light flashed on, Clark tossed the dog's corpse into a bush and ran.

Dangerous. So dangerous.

He sat down beside Trisha on the brown leather couch. His fingers tapped the soft couch arm.

I'm out of control, he thought.

I'm so thirsty, I can't sit still.

He raised his eyes from her throat. "Do you want to go out?" he asked, forcing his voice to come out low and steady.

Trisha frowned thoughtfully. "No. I don't think so. I tried to call you. I—I'm really not in the mood to do anything. I had a weird experience. On Fear Street."

"What do you mean?" he asked, licking his lips. "What happened?"

She hesitated. She seemed about to tell him something. But he could see her change her mind.

"I—I can't stop thinking about graduation rehearsal," she replied finally. "That was so frightening. So unbelievably frightening."

"Yes," Clark agreed, nodding sympathetically. "I can't stop thinking about it, either."

But a nice, long drink would help me forget.

"I think I'm afraid to go out," Trisha confessed, tensely curling and uncurling a strand of blond hair between her fingers. "I mean, I'm totally freaked."

Are we alone? Clark wondered, leaning toward her. Is anyone else in the house?

Yes. He heard footsteps in the hallway. The sound of a vacuum cleaner from somewhere upstairs.

Trisha's family had so many servants. Trisha was never alone.

"I think we should go for a long drive," Clark suggested.

Trisha shook her head and squeezed his hand apologetically. "No. Really. I don't think so."

"Then how about a movie?" Clark hoped she couldn't see how desperate he was. "You know, a movie would really take both of our minds off what happened."

Then later we can be alone somewhere. . . .

He wiped a spot of drool off his lower lip. Had she noticed it? No.

I need to drink, he thought. I'm going crazy!

"It's a bad time," Trisha said, lowering her eyes. "I'm sorry, Clark. Really."

He had to plead with her. He nearly begged.

Finally she agreed to the movie.

How did he ever drive there without crashing the car?

What movie did they see? He couldn't remember. He spent the whole two hours gazing at Trisha's throat.

Afterward, he wanted to drive to the river "to talk." But Trisha announced that she was starving.

They sat across from each other in a booth

at Alma's Coffee Shop. He watched her gulp down a cheeseburger and fries. He nibbled at a grilled cheese sandwich.

Food repulsed him.

How could he think about food with that fresh, warm blood flowing across the table from him?

How could he *think*?

He realized she had asked him a question. He hadn't heard a word. "What?"

She took a long sip of her Diet Coke. "Do you think Josie and Josh will still have their graduation party tomorrow night?"

Clark shrugged. "I guess."

"Tomorrow night is the party, and the next day is graduation," Trisha said. "Do you believe it?"

"I can't wait to get it all over with," Clark replied, gazing at the throbbing veins in her throat. "I'll be so happy if we finally make it through graduation."

"They *can't* cancel graduation," Trisha declared. "They *can't*. It just wouldn't be fair to all of us. We've been through so much. We deserve our graduation."

"Yeah," Clark replied, barely hearing a word.

He drove them to the river. He parked in a dark spot hidden by a clump of tall trees.

Had he ever felt this thirsty before? This *needy*?

He couldn't remember. He couldn't think.

He slid an arm around her and pulled her close.

Did she resist?

No.

She rested her head on his shoulder.

He smelled the flowery fragrance of her hair. He smelled the blood.

So tangy, so sweet.

He could smell it. He could *hear* it, pouring through her veins.

"Nice here," she murmured. "Peaceful."

His eyes moved from her smile to her pulsing throat.

He turned to her. He couldn't hold back any longer.

He lowered his face to her neck.

He could feel the tingling in his gums, the sharp tingling that he always felt as his fangs slid down. Slid down over his drooling lips, over his chin.

He opened his mouth wide—and lowered his fangs to her throat.

Clark Drinks

A flash of white light.
Headlights?
No. The light swept over the front
seat of the car. Stopped at Clark's face.

"Huh?" He raised an arm, shielding himself
from its painful brightness.

He sat up with a jerk, his fangs sliding up
into his mouth.

Trisha pulled away, straightening her hair.

Swallowing, Clark turned to the light. And
saw a face peering into the open car window.

He saw the face. Saw the stern expression.
Then he saw the uniform cap. The dark uniform. The badge.

The police officer lowered his flashlight.
"You'd better move on," he growled.

Clark blinked, trying to force the spots of
lingering light from his eyes. "We weren't
doing anything, Officer."

"This isn't a good spot," the policeman insisted, his face inches from Clark's. Clark could see tiny beads of sweat on the man's sideburns. "It isn't safe, kids. There's been a lot of strangeness around. Move on, okay?"

I'm so thirsty, Clark thought. This can't be happening.

He had no choice. He leaned forward over the wheel. Swallowing. His throat so dry, so achingly dry.

His hand trembled as he turned the key in the ignition and started up the car. The police officer watched him back the car up, then drive away.

"Uh . . . let's go up to River Ridge," he suggested. A lot of kids parked at River Ridge. It was usually crowded, but he figured he could find a private spot. He wiped a spot of drool off his chin.

"It's kind of late," Trisha sighed. "You'd better drive me home."

"Are you sure?" he asked, unable to hide his disappointment.

She had slid against the passenger door, far from him now. She kept her eyes straight ahead, her expression cold.

"It's not that late," he protested. "We could—"

"No. Really," she insisted. "That cop is right. There's too much strangeness around." She shuddered.

Clark uttered a long sigh. His tongue slid over his dry lips.

Dry . . . I'm so dry.

Trisha hugged herself tightly, her eyes shut now.

I have no choice, Clark thought bitterly. I have to drive her home.

He switched on the radio to cover the silence. As he turned the car around, he swallowed hard. So dry. My mouth is so dry. I really need to drink.

A few minutes later he pulled the car through the gates at the front of Trisha's mansion. The tires crunched over the gravel as the car eased up to the house.

Dry as gravel, Clark thought. My throat feels as if it's filled with stones.

He cut the engine and clicked off the headlights.

I have to drink!

Whirling around, he made a desperate grab for Trisha.

But she had already pushed open the car door and was climbing out.

"Trisha—" Clark gasped. His throat ached. His cry came out in a raspy whisper.

He jumped out of the car and hurried to catch up to her on the walk. A light flashed on in the front window. A servant peered out from the living room.

"I'm sorry," Trisha murmured, turning to him. Her blond hair fluttered in the wind. She placed a hand on his sleeve. "Sorry I freaked out like that. But . . . it's all just too frightening."

Clark opened his mouth to reply. But a startled gasp escaped his throat as he felt something brush against his leg.

He jumped back—and saw a black kitten at his feet.

"Minnie—what are you doing out so early?" Trisha called down to the cat. She turned back to Clark. "That's our new kitten. We usually don't put Minnie out until we close up for the night."

Clark lifted the cat into his arms and petted it gently. "She's so cute." He stroked the kitten's dark fur. "So cute."

He was still petting the kitten when Trisha said good night and disappeared into the house.

The door closed behind her. The porch light went out.

The servant had disappeared from the front window.

"Nice kitty," Clark whispered, petting it gently. "Nice kitty."

He raised the kitten to his face and sank his fangs into its soft, warm belly.

The cat let out a startled cry and kicked out its legs, struggling to escape.

But Clark held on.

He buried his face in the kitten's belly and drank . . . drank thirstily . . . noisily . . . drank it dry . . . warm blood splashing over his chin, his cheeks. He drank . . . finally drank.

Chapter Twenty-five

Kill the Vampire!

Josh ripped open a bag of tortilla chips. He poured the chips into a bowl and set it down next to the bowl of salsa.

He sighed and raised his eyes to Josie, who was stretching on tiptoes to tape red and white streamers across the living-room mirror. "I can't believe we're going ahead with this party," he said, shaking his head. "No one will come. Everyone is too scared."

Josie finished taping the streamers and stepped back to admire them. "I told you, I think we're all going to be okay," she said. She set the tape dispenser down. "I don't think there's anything to be afraid of now."

Josh groaned. "How can you say that? You were there at graduation rehearsal. You saw those ghouls—"

"Trisha and I—we . . . did something," Josie interrupted. "I don't want to talk about

167

it now. But we did something to protect the senior class. We got help."

Josh set two large bottles of Coke on the food table. He narrowed his eyes at his step-sister. "Help? What kind of help?"

"There isn't time to explain," Josie replied, glancing at the mantel clock. "Everyone will be here in an hour. Did you pull out some dance CDs? I think we should push these chairs against the wall."

Josh sighed again. "No one is going to feel like dancing," he murmured. "We all just want to make it through graduation alive."

"Listen to me, Josh—" Josie started.

But the front doorbell rang. And the door burst open before she could make a move to answer it. Trisha came running in breath-lessly, followed by a pale, sweating Matty Winger.

"Hey, guys—" Josh started.

Trisha brushed past him and crossed the room to Josie. "I—I've been trying to reach you all day!" she cried, gasping for breath. "Your phone is off the hook or something."

Josie took a step back. "What's wrong?"

"I have a reality check—about Clark," Trisha declared.

"He's a vampire!" Matty chimed in.

Josie's mouth dropped open.

"All those rumors about him—they're *true*!" Trisha exclaimed. "I—I went out with him last night—and he tried to bite my throat."

Josie swallowed hard. "Trisha—are you sure? Maybe he was just kidding around or—?"

"I saw his fangs. A policeman showed up and stopped him just in time. I made him drive me home. This morning I found Minnie, my new kitten. She was dead on the front lawn. I saw two puncture holes in her stomach, and . . . and . . ."

Trisha covered her mouth and turned her head away. Her shoulders rocked up and down. Josie hurried to comfort her.

"Trisha is telling the truth," Matty told them. "Clark is a vampire. He's been drinking my blood."

"Whoa—!" A cry escaped Josh's open mouth. "No way!"

Matty nodded. Sweat rolled down his round cheeks. "Clark tried to cloud my mind so I wouldn't remember. But it didn't entirely work. The memory forced its way to my mind. He—he's been drinking my blood. That's why I've felt so horrible for days!"

"Oh, wow," Josh murmured, shaking his head. "Wow. What are we going to do?"

Josie still had her arm around Trisha's shoulders. Trisha wiped tears off her cheeks and stepped away. "We have to kill him," she said through gritted teeth. "We have to kill the vampire."

Josie stared at her but didn't reply.

"Don't you see?" Trisha continued, her voice high and trembling. "Clark may be the cause of all the horrible things that have happened to our class. Maybe it was the vampire's evil that killed our friends. And *not* the evil of the Fears!"

Her eyes burned into Josie's. "Maybe you've been blaming yourself for nothing, Josie. Maybe the evil came from Clark—not from a spirit you called up."

"I—I don't know," Josie stammered. "Do you really think Clark's evil is strong enough to kill so many people in our class?"

"It doesn't matter," Matty declared. "The vampire has to die. I want to pay Clark back for what he's done to me. For what he's done to all of us."

"Wh-what are you going to do?" Josie asked.

"You'll see," Matty replied. He turned and crossed to the front door. He pulled the door open, then turned back into the room. "Call him, Trisha," he ordered. "Call Clark."

"Huh?" Trisha gasped. "I can't!"

"Call him," Matty insisted, motioning to the phone on the coffee table. "Get him over here now. Before the party starts. I'll take care of the rest."

He disappeared outside, closing the door behind him.

Josie placed a hand on Trisha's trembling shoulder. "Go ahead. You can do it," she said, her voice just above a whisper. "He'll come running over here if you ask him to."

"But—I'm really scared," Trisha replied.

"Where did Matty go?" Josh asked. "What is he planning to do?"

As if in reply, the front door swung open. Matty appeared carrying a slender wooden fence post. "I hope you don't mind. I pulled it off the fence at the side of your house."

"A wooden stake?" Josie cried, raising her hand to her mouth.

Matty nodded. "Your father has a workshop in the basement, right?" He touched the pointed tip. "I want to file it down. Make it as sharp as I can."

"You're really going to kill him?" Josh demanded.

"He's not a human. He's a vampire," Matty replied grimly. "He has to die. He'd kill us all if he had a chance. Look what he's done to me."

He turned to Trisha. "Did you call him?"

Trisha hesitated, then grabbed up the phone. "I'm doing it now."

Matty disappeared into the basement.

A few seconds later Trisha had Clark on the line. "Clark, how are you? I'm at Josie's," she said in a whisper.

Josie stood close beside Trisha, but she couldn't hear Clark's reply.

"I've been thinking about last night," Trisha breathed into the phone. She gripped the receiver so tightly, her hand was white. "I'd like to see you, Clark. Can you come to Josie's? Can you come to the party early?"

Trisha bit her lip as she listened to Clark's

reply. She nodded to Josie, signaling that Clark had agreed to come. "Great. See you in a few minutes," she said, before hanging up.

She let out a long sigh and slumped onto the couch. "He's coming," she reported. "Now what?"

"Leave him to me," Matty said, returning to the living room. He slapped the wooden stake against his hand. "Just leave him to me."

Josh and Trisha were hiding when Clark arrived a few minutes later. Josie opened the door to him. "Clark—hi." She tried to sound calm, nonchalant.

Clark was dressed all in black, as usual. His eyes surveyed the room. "Is Trisha here?" he asked, unable to hide his eagerness. "She called me."

"Yeah. Sure. She's in the den," Josie replied. She pointed to the closed den door across the hall.

She knew Matty was waiting in there. Waiting in the dark with his wooden stake. Waiting to be alone with the vampire, to take his revenge, to drive the stake deep into Count Clarkula's cold, cold heart.

Clark licked his lips eagerly. He brushed past Josie, taking long strides to the den.

Josie shivered. Clark's touch sent a chill down her entire body.

She realized she was holding her breath. Trembling. She wrapped her arms around herself, held herself tight.

She watched Clark pull open the den door and step into the darkened room. "Trisha—?" he called.

Can Matty do it? Josie wondered.

Can Matty really drive that stake through Clark's chest?

She didn't have long to think about it.

A few seconds after Clark stepped into the den, a high wail rang out.

A scream. Of shock. Of pain.

Josie covered her ears. Pressed her hands tightly against the side of her face, trying to shut out the terrifying cry.

Is that Clark screaming? she wondered.

Or is it Matty?

Chapter Twenty-six

Party Time

The cry of agony rose and fell like a siren. And then a deep silence fell over the house.

Josie stared at the closed den door.

Trisha and Josh reappeared from the hall. "Who screamed?" Josh demanded. "Was it Clark?"

"Did Matty kill him?" Trisha demanded, her voice shrill, frantic, her hands balled into tensed fists at her sides.

Josie shrugged. And held her gaze on the door.

Finally it opened. Matty staggered out, shaken, breathing hard, his chest heaving up and down. "I . . . I killed the vampire," he announced.

Josie breathed a long sigh, of horror and relief. Trisha slumped back against the wall and shut her eyes. Josh stared open-mouthed as Matty dropped heavily onto the couch.

"Clark is . . . dead?" Josie choked out.

Matty nodded. "I shoved the stake into his chest. He screamed. He wasn't expecting it. He . . . he didn't move or anything. I shoved the stake in, and he just crumbled."

"Crumbled? What do you mean?" Josh asked.

"He crumbled," Matty repeated, still breathing hard. "His skin—it fell off. His bones, *too*. Everything. He just crumbled to ashes. Just a pile of ashes. And then the ashes disappeared."

"You mean—there's nothing in there?" Josh asked, pointing to the den.

Matty nodded. "Nothing left. The vampire is dead."

A smile slowly spread over Josh's face. He turned to Josie. "I guess that means it's party time."

No one really felt like partying. Even Mickey Myers, who could usually be counted on to be the rowdiest member of any crowd, sat quietly by the fireplace, his head down, sipping from a can of Coke.

Josie kept the music cranked up high. Jennifer Fear tried to get Kenny Klein to dance with her. But Kenny shouted an excuse and turned away.

"Hey, guys—we've made it! We're all going to graduate tomorrow!" Stacy Malcolm declared.

"Not all of us made it," Dana Palmer muttered bitterly.

Her words sent a stab of pain through Josie's chest. Dana wasn't the only one who missed her twin sister, Deirdre. Josie missed Deirdre, *too*. Missed her every day.

I'm so surprised Dana came to the party, Josie thought. She is so sad and depressed. I guess she just didn't want to be alone tonight on the night before graduation.

I guess that's why most everyone came.

"What a lame party," Josh whispered to Josie. "Mom and Dad didn't have to go hide out at Aunt Lisa's. The party isn't noisy or wild at all."

Josie sighed. "I knew this would happen."

"Hey—where's Clark?" someone shouted over the music. "Where's Count Clarkula?"

"I killed him!" Matty declared.

Most everyone laughed.

Of course, no one believed Matty was telling the truth.

Josie shivered. Someone had been murdered right in her own house. Just minutes before the party.

Of course, Clark wasn't a human. He was a vampire. Probably a thousand years old.

But every time Josie passed the den, she felt a chill at the back of her neck. She wondered if she'd ever get over it.

Will any of us ever be able to get over the horror of this year? she asked herself.

"How's it going?" Jennifer's soft voice broke

into Josie's troubled thoughts.

Josie shrugged. "Maybe this party wasn't such a good idea."

"We don't have much to celebrate," Jennifer replied. She took a long sip from her soda can. "If we survive tomorrow, then maybe we can—"

"We'll survive," Josie interrupted, squeezing her friend's hand.

Jennifer's eyes widened in surprise.

"I have a lot to tell you," Josie confided. "I haven't had a chance. But so much has happened. Trisha and I—we went to the old Simon Fear mansion. We did something there. Something to save the class. It was very frightening, but—"

"What?" Jennifer demanded eagerly. "What did you do?"

Josie took a deep breath. "Stay after the party," she pleaded. "I'll ask Trisha to stay, too. We'll tell you everything. You won't believe it, but—"

"I'll believe it," Jennifer replied, rolling her eyes. "After this horrible year, I'll believe anything."

Josie let out a scream as the front door burst open.

A blast of wind, louder than the dance music, hurled into the room. A vase toppled over. A painting fell heavily off the wall.

The cold wind swirled around the room.

Some kids screamed in surprise. Others fell silent.

The music stopped abruptly.

"Who opened the door?" Josie heard Trisha cry.

Another powerful blast of wind sent the soda cans and food toppling off the table. The roar drowned out the clatter of cans and bowls dropping against the floor.

A soda can rolled against Josie's shoe. She stumbled over it as she took a step toward the door.

And stopped when she saw the long red cloak.

The cloak with its scarlet hood.

The skeletal hands poking out from under the heavy robe.

The cloak flapped loudly in the swirling cold wind. The hood fell back, revealing the grinning skull. The sunken eyes. The cracked and missing teeth in the yellowed jaw.

Josie grabbed the wall as her knees collapsed beneath her.

The evil spirit.

Josie knew all along that it would return. And now the moment had arrived.

The cloaked figure raised its bony hands high, as if about to fly. It turned and trained its empty eye sockets on Josie.

"*You called me forth*," the evil spirit rasped. "*You performed the Doom Spell to bring me here. Now I have come to finish my job.*"

Chapter Twenty-seven

"I Summon Thee Again!"

Josie uttered a cry of terror. She collapsed to her knees. As she hit the floor, pain shot up her body.

Gazing around, she saw Stacy duck behind the couch. She saw two girls crying by the fireplace. Mickey and Dana clung to each other, held each other tightly, their faces twisted in terror.

Josie saw Josh freeze behind the food table. Matty sat in an armchair, leaning forward stiffly, blinking, blinking his eyes rapidly, as if trying to blink the hideous sight away.

At the back wall Josie saw Jennifer struggling to pry open the window. The window wouldn't move. Jennifer tugged and strained frantically.

Kids cried and screamed.

And then, as Josie gazed at them in horror, they all started to fade. The screaming, twisted, terrified faces all faded behind a thick screen of gray smoke.

The smoke, billowing, choking, foul-smelling, rose up through the room, rose up from the floor, formed a thick curtain.

Shadows flickered on the smoke curtain. And as Josie stared, still on her knees, unable to move, unable to scream or cry out, as she stared into the billowing smoke, she saw the flickering shadows become solid, saw faces form—the faces of her friends.

Projected onto the smoke, as if on a movie screen, Josie saw her friends now, saw everyone in the room.

Unable to move. Unable to scream.

She stared in silent horror as the Evil Spirit raised his skeletal hands. Made the figures dance on the screen of smoke.

Made them bend and twist and howl.

And then he showed Josie what he planned to do to each of her friends.

Josie wanted to shut her eyes. Wanted to turn away. Wanted to jump up and run.

But she hunched there, paralyzed, on her knees. And watched the evil creature murder her friends one by one on the screen.

Watched him rip off Jennifer's arms, wrap them around her throat, and strangle her with them. Watched him twist Stacy's head until her neck cracked and her head bobbed lifelessly like a deflated balloon.

Watched him shove a bony hand down Josh's throat—deeper, deeper—and pull up

Josh's wet, glowing red and yellow insides, pull them right out through his open mouth.

Watched him crush Mickey's head between his skeletal hands. Watched him poke out Trisha's eyeballs and stick his bony fingers through her empty eye sockets deep into her brain.

Josie watched the gruesome spectacle on the screen of smoke, as if watching a disgusting slasher movie.

Trembling, whimpering softly to herself, she knew this was no movie. This was a preview of what the evil spirit planned.

The gray smoke billowed, thicker, thicker. And as Josie stared, the torn, tortured, dying figures faded away.

"It's time," Josie murmured out loud.

I have to act now, she decided. If I don't, we will all die just as he showed us.

Leaning against the wall for support, she struggled to her feet. "Spirit—!" she cried. But her voice came out so tiny and weak, even she wasn't sure she had spoken.

She sucked in a deep breath of sour, smoky air. "Spirit—!" she called, louder this time.

Half-hidden in the red cloak, the yellowed skull turned its empty eye sockets on her. Inside the deep holes, Josie could see the twin snake heads peering out at her.

"Spirit—" she called. "I have a surprise for you. You will not be able to finish your job here tonight!"

The evil creature opened its jaws in a roar

of protest. The twin snakes leaped out, jaws snapping furiously.

"Trisha and I brought another spirit out from the grave!" Josie told it. "A spirit that will *destroy* you!"

Josie didn't wait for the spirit to react again. She remembered Henry Conrad's instructions clearly. Standing in front of Simon Fear's burned-out mansion, he had told her: "Shout the words *I summon thee* three times, and I will be there."

Her heart pounded so hard, she could barely breathe. Her whole body shook violently.

Shout the words, she instructed herself.

Forget your fear. This is your last chance. Shout the words!

She took a deep breath. Opened her mouth. Screamed, "I summon thee!" once.

And the twin snakes stretched from the evil skeleton's eye sockets—and plunged into her open mouth.

Chapter Twenty-eight

The Rescue

The dry, warm snake bodies slid over her tongue, brushed against the roof of her mouth.

Josie choked. Fell back against the wall.

The yellowed skull leaned over her. The two snakes slid out farther from the empty eye sockets. Josie could feel the snakes easing down the back of her throat.

She gagged.

Her whole body heaved, and she vomited violently.

The force of the vomit sent the snakes flying out in retreat. Startled, they bobbed in front of her face as she retched.

My one last chance, she realized.

Choking, sputtering, she could still feel the disgusting touch of the snakes slithering down her throat.

Struggling to ignore her horror, she dropped flat to the floor. Rolled quickly behind the evil, cloaked figure.

And opened her mouth in a desperate cry: "I summon thee! I summon thee! I summon thee!"

A deafening roar seemed to shake the house.

Her friends shrieked and cried. All a blur to her. A blur of dark colors, frightened faces.

Struggling to focus her eyes, Josie turned to see the front door fly open.

A tall figure strode quickly into the room.

Henry Conrad!

Yes! He wore the same old-fashioned black suit. His blond hair tumbled over his forehead. His eyes shone like dark lights, glaring across the still-smoky room at the evil spirit.

The skeletal figure took a step back, wrapping his cloak around him with his bony hands. The twin snakes pulled back into the skull.

Josie struggled to her feet. "You're here!" she choked out.

Henry Conrad ignored her cry. He stepped past her, his dark features set in a furious scowl, his eyes locked on the retreating evil spirit.

Josie turned to the cloaked skeleton, watching it retreat. "Now you will die!" she cried. "The Doom Spell will end. Now *you* are doomed!"

Henry Conrad walked steadily, moving

toward his foe. His glowing, dark eyes didn't blink. His features remained frozen, calm. His arms were lowered stiffly at his sides, hands opening and closing, opening and closing, as if preparing for a fight.

The evil spirit backed against a bookshelf. Now it tilted its yellowed head and stared open-jawed at the advancing figure of Henry Conrad.

Henry stopped inches in front of the cloaked skeleton. Still staring hard into the dark, empty eye sockets. Still pumping his hands open and shut.

And then, to Josie's surprise, Henry turned his back on the spirit. Turned to face Josie and her friends.

And as he turned, his face began to change. The skin melted, dropped off in chunks. The blond hair fell to the floor in a clump. The flesh flaked off his hands, revealing yellowed bone underneath.

"No!" Josie wailed. "Nooooooo!"

Her horrified cry rose up over the cries of the other seniors.

Henry Conrad's face melted away, revealing a yellowed, grinning skull underneath. His dark eyes flashed at Josie one last time, and then slid out of their sockets, fell, and bounced silently across the floor.

"Nooooooooo!" Josie wailed. "Noooo—please!"

Henry stared at her with empty eye sockets now. Chunks of teeth toppled from his jaw.

"You—you're both the same!" Josie heard Trisha cry out.

It was true. Twin skeletons.

"You tricked us!" Trisha cried. "You only pretended to be my great-grandfather!"

The skeletons moved quickly. They bounded forward. Hit each other head-on.

And slid together.

Melted . . . melted into each other.

Melted until only one skeleton remained.

"We are one and the same!" the evil creature bellowed in a deep animal roar. "Why would we fight each other?"

"No—please—" Josie choked out, her entire body trembling, shaking so hard, she could barely stand. "Please—"

"You have only strengthened me!" the spirit boomed. "You have doubled my power. And now it is time—now you will all die!"

Chapter Twenty-nine

Matty Is a Liar

The skeleton's red cloak fluttered in a strong, cold blast of wind. It raised its bony hands high and tossed back its head in triumph.

Trembling in terror, Josie slid against the wall until she bumped into Josh. She grabbed his hands and squeezed. They hugged each other as the evil skeleton floated toward them.

"I tried . . ." Josie murmured. "But the evil spirit tricked us. He tricked us."

"I—I don't understand," Josh stammered, holding onto her.

"It doesn't matter," Josie sighed, letting the tears roll down her burning cheeks. "We're all going to die."

Another blast of frozen air made everyone cry out in shock. The skeleton's red cloak flapped and billowed like a giant pennant.

He advanced toward Jennifer Fear. His bony fingers crackled as he lowered his hands to Jennifer's throat.

Josie gasped when she saw the den door fly open. It slammed hard against the wall.

The evil spirit turned at the sound. Everyone turned.

Josie uttered a startled cry as Clark came bursting out from the den.

Her cry ended abruptly. The room grew silent.

As Clark made his way into the living room, the evil spirit pulled his hands back from Jennifer's throat and retreated a step, his cloak billowing around him.

"Clark is alive!" Trisha screamed. "Matty— you lied! You lied to us!"

Clark's dark eyes scanned the room. He spread his arms—and floated off the floor.

He turned to Josie. Smiled a cruel smile. And she saw sharp, curled fangs slide down from his open mouth.

"No—!" Josie gasped. "Clark—what are you doing? What are you going to do?"

Chapter Thirty

Two Vampires

Screams rang out as Clark floated off the floor. Floated higher, his arms spread. Floated until he hovered over the evil spirit.

The cloaked figure pulled back, tried to twist away from the floating vampire.

His eyes on the two figures, Matty backed away, backed away until he bumped into Josie.

"You lied to us," she gasped. "You didn't kill him."

Matty's eyes burned into Josie's. "I couldn't kill him!" he declared. "Because . . . Clark made me a vampire, too!"

Josie fell back against the wall as Matty stretched out his arms, lowered his fangs—and floated off the floor.

Side by side, Matty and Clark hovered over the evil spirit.

"Our evil rules!" Clark cried. "The evil of the immortal—the ancient evil of the vampire—is older and more powerful than the evil of this paltry spirit!"

Clark gave a signal. And he and Matty both swooped down on the cloaked skeleton together.

They battered him to the floor.

The skeleton uttered a groan of protest.

The snakes shot up from his eye sockets. Stabbed at the two vampires. Stabbed hard. Stabbed again, jaws snapping loudly.

But Clark and Matty were too strong, their evil too powerful.

Clark grabbed the darting snakes, one in each hand—and ripped them from the skull.

Matty took the skull in both hands. And with a triumphant cry, tore the skull off the evil creature's shoulders.

The skull let out a shrill shriek. Crying out its fury between Matty's hands.

With a groan Matty pulled his arm back—and heaved the shrieking skull out the open door.

The headless skeleton rose up. Leaped out from under the red cloak.

But Matty and Clark crushed it between them. Crushed the rib cage. Crushed the bones. Crushed them to powder.

The yellow powder swirled in a gust of cold wind. It swirled around the two vampires. Then floated over Kenny Klein.

Kenny gasped and fell onto his back,

knocked over by the weight of the swirling bone powder.

Frozen in terror, Josie watched the curtain of powder rise up, up over them all. Then fall silently to the floor like a yellow snowfall.

"It's gone! The evil spirit is dead!" Josie choked out.

Silence now. No one wanted to speak. Still gripped in panic, no one made a sound.

Josie took a step forward to thank Clark and Matty.

But before she could utter a word, the two boys began to change.

They spun furiously on the floor, kicking up swirls of yellow bone powder.

Spinning, spinning frantically, they began to shrink. To darken. To change.

When they stopped spinning, their human bodies had vanished. They were wide-winged black bats, red eyes glowing.

Chittering loudly, a shrill farewell cry, they flapped their silky, dark wings—and floated out the open door.

Silence again.

Shocked silence.

And then everyone realized at once that the danger was over.

They were finally safe. The curse had been lifted.

Clark Dickson and Matty Winger—of all people!—had saved the class.

Cries rang out—happy this time.

Hugs. Tears of joy.

Weeping and laughing at the same time, the seniors clung to each other.

"It's over," they murmured.

"We made it. We're going to graduate."

"We're alive. We're safe."

Josie hugged Trisha tightly, pressed her tear-wet cheek against Trisha's. "We're okay," she whispered. "We're okay."

They both turned and hugged Josh. "We survived!" Josie cried. "Now we can graduate in peace."

Kenny Klein spun Josie around and hugged her. "Of course we can!" he cried. "Of course we can!"

Tears running down her face, Josie gazed around the room at her joyful friends. Only a few hours till graduation, she thought.

Will we really be okay?

Chapter Thirty-one

Graduation

"Is the cap okay? It's tilted," Josie complained.

Trisha straightened a pleat in her graduation robe. Then she turned and helped Josie with her cap.

"It keeps sliding down over my forehead," Josie complained.

Trisha laughed. "Do you *believe* that our only worry today is how we look in our caps and gowns!"

Josie laughed, too, and hugged Trisha. Both of their caps fell to the floor.

They were still laughing and joking happily as the music started. Josie put on her solemn face as the seniors began to march down the aisles of the auditorium.

She crossed her fingers and said a silent prayer. Please, please, let everything go okay today. Please let us graduate. Let the curse on our class be over.

As she followed the line of seniors, she kept glancing nervously back to the door-ways.

Would the ghoulish parade of dead seniors repeat itself?

Would the graduation ceremony be ruined by ghouls or skeletons or vampires?

Josie took her seat onstage as the music stopped. The sound of rustling gowns and scraping chairs filled the auditorium.

Josie searched for Clark and Matty. But their chairs were empty.

The principal stepped to the podium to begin the ceremony.

Josie kept returning her eyes to the doors at the back.

Who will enter? Who will burst in to ruin our graduation?

She didn't hear the principal's speech. Or the two songs by the Shadyside High choir. She heard only a few words and phrases of the guest speaker's graduation talk.

"The future is yours . . ." he kept saying.

Yes, it is, Josie thought. We actually *have* a future.

The evil is gone . . . gone forever.

She had seen his head ripped off and tossed away. His bones broken into a fine powder.

Josie forced herself to pay attention as Kenny Klein made his way to the podium to deliver his valedictorian speech.

Kenny spoke well and with emotion. It took only a few minutes for him to have everyone in tears.

"We not only say good-bye to Shadyside High today," Kenny declared. "We also say good-bye to many good friends who are not graduating with us today."

Sobs rang out as Kenny began naming the seniors who had not survived. "Good-bye, Danielle," Kenny said, his voice lowering to nearly a whisper. "Good-bye, Jade. Good-bye, Gary. Good-bye, Deirdre . . ."

Everyone was crying now. Josie didn't even try to stop the tears that flowed down her cheeks. It was all so sad. And yet it felt good to cry today. Cleansing.

We really are saying good-bye to our friends—and good-bye to all our sadness, she thought.

"Good-bye, Ty. Good-bye, Phoebe," Kenny said, finishing his list. His voice cracked, and he choked back a sob. "Let us all bow our heads now," Kenny requested, his voice quivering with emotion. "And let each of us say good-bye silently to our good friends."

Trying to get control and stop her sobs, Josie lowered her head and shut her eyes.

It's okay, she told herself.

Everything is going to be okay from now on.

Silence fell heavily over the auditorium. No one moved. No one coughed.

And then the silent good-byes were over.

The seniors were asked to stand. Two men wheeled a table stacked high with diplomas next to the principal's podium.

He began calling out names, handing out diplomas. Applause rang out through the auditorium at the announcement of each name.

Such joyful applause.

Josie could see her parents sitting near the middle of the auditorium. They both had beaming smiles on their faces.

It's happening, Josie thought gratefully.

We're graduating. We're all finally graduating.

When she stepped forward and received her diploma, she squeezed it so hard her hand ached.

The ceremony ended with two more songs by the choir.

The applause shook the auditorium.

Grinning happily, her heart pounding, Josie hurried backstage to drop off her cap and gown.

"Hey—" she cried out as a hand grabbed her by the arm and tugged her aside. "Kenny?"

Kenny Klein raised a finger to his lips. "Sshh. Wait a second, Josie. I want to show you something." He pulled her to the side curtain, away from the crowd of laughing, chattering seniors.

"Huh? Kenny? What is it?" Josie asked.

"Watch," Kenny replied.

"Watch what?" she demanded impatiently. "I've got to go. My parents—"

She stopped in midsentence as Kenny started to change.

The top of his head split open with a loud *craaaack*. His graduation cap dropped to the floor.

The two sides of his face fell away, like a rubber mask split in two.

Two long, slender snakes arched up over the collar of his gown.

The snakes wound themselves around Kenny's exposed skull.

The skull snapped its jaws once, twice. Kenny's eyeballs rolled out and bounced onto the floor. *Thud, thud*.

Josie raised her hands to her cheeks and screamed.

"*Kenny isn't here anymore!*" the skeletal figure bellowed at her in an ugly, inhuman rasp.

He lowered his face to hers. Closer . . . so close she could smell his putrid breath.

"*Kenny had to say good-bye, too! But he loaned me this splendid new body yesterday. It's time for me to finish my work. Happy Graduation, Josie!*"

R.L. Stine
Seniors
a FEAR STREET® series

AVAILABLE FROM GOLD KEY® PAPERBACKS:

FEAR STREET® Sagas

FEAR STREET® titles

AVAILABLE FROM GOLD KEY® PAPERBACKS:

About R.L. Stine

R.L. Stine is the best-selling author in America. He has written more than one hundred scary books for young people, all of them bestsellers.

His series include *Fear Street*, *Fear Street Seniors*, and the *Fear Street Sagas*.

Bob grew up in Columbus, Ohio. Today he lives in New York City with his wife, Jane, his son, Matt, and his dog, Nadine.

Do you know the address for Fear?

www.fearstreet.com

Connect to the curse of **The Fear Family** with the brand new **Fear Street Website**! This scary site brings you up close and personal with the legend of the Fears and their legacy of blood. With sneak peeks of upcoming stories, top secret information, games, gossip, and the latest buzz from R.L. Stine on who will survive, this is your chance to know the deadly truth.

Get caught in the web of fear!